Marigold Dark

Marigold Dark
Copyright: Paul Bisson
Published: 10th March 2015
Publisher: Jayplate

The right of Paul Bisson to be identified as author of this Work has been asserted by him in accordance with sections 77 and 78 of the Copyright, Designs and Patents Act 1988.

All rights reserved. No part of this publication may be reproduced, stored in retrieval system, copied in any form or by any means, electronic, mechanical, photocopying, recording or otherwise transmitted without written permission from the publisher. You must not circulate this book in any format.

French at heart though British by choice, the Channel Islands sit a mere (though always amiable) stone's throw from the western edge of Normandy. Jersey is the largest and most southerly of these.

Viewed from above, the island is a patchwork of greens punctuated by varying bursts of residential sprawl, all bound by forty-eight miles of rugged coastline. The view from below very much depends on where you are standing and what you happen to be doing at the time.

Split into twelve parishes, Jersey's capital and commercial centre St Helier is located on the southern coast; comparisons with any other corporatised mid-sized English town are fair.

At the last count the island boasted a population of just under one hundred thousand souls. Not all of these work in Finance.

The Nazis made it over for a while during the war, though they've not been seen since.

The French for toad is *crapaud*, a term that is sometimes humorously applied by Jersey folk to themselves.

This is all you need to know.

PB

I should have been a pair of ragged claws
Scuttling across the floors of silent seas.

The Love Song of J. Alfred Prufrock, T.S. Eliot

Chapters

1 - Rise and Shine
2 - Pillow Talk
3 - Things Take a Dive
4 - Non-Attack of the Half Naked Cyborg Assassin
5 - Cell Fun
6 - Lobster
7 - Cauliflower Omelette
8 - Salma
9 - Dealing in the Dark
10 - Taxi For Two
11 - The Folly of Moses Corbet
12 - Towering
13 - Inferno
14 - Driving Test
15 - Stuff
16 - Tick, Glock
17 - Looking Glass
18 - Old Chum
19 - The Bona Fide Bastard
20 - A Little Bit Flat
21 - Bits and Babs
22 - Off to Work We Go
23 - The Earth Moves
24 - Twist

1 – Rise and Shine

The punches keep on coming.
Thwack. Thwunk. Thwabber.
I'm in my old office swivel chair, wrists bound numb to the armrests with strips of brightly coloured fabric; a selection of Tie Rack's finest nooses from my office days, cruelly reassigned to arms and ankles. I'd put in a request to have them loosened, though I'm not sure who to ask.

Aside from my bindings I'm naked, naturally.

Thwok. Each blow sends me spinning full circle into my attacker's next swing, so that any diminishing of rotational momentum is quickly countered by the impact of his fist against my jaw. *Thwudder.*

Quite a chair this one, if I remember rightly. My Old Faithful; lockable tilt mechanism, gas seat height adjustment, sturdy chrome base, the works. A real decade-guzzling, life-stealing, burgundy fabric beast of a chair. Spent my thirties counting numbers for Malcolm and crew in this baby, servicing the columns of the wealthy, ticking rich men's boxes, ticking their tax liabilities until they giggled and squealed.

Someone's clearly oiled the bearings; I don't remember it spinning quite as well as this. Don't remember owning all these shifting technicolor ties, either. And as for my assailant, that suited fellow with the furious face? Nope.

And then things slow down a little and I realise that it's my suit that he's wearing. And that's my face. And he's *me*.

It's a dream of course, a fact from which I draw only partial relief as I pop naked and sobbing into an unfamiliar bed. Wakefulness assaults me with the usual BLAM! of parched pain as I take in the mean and cluttered room, the low ceiling mapped with mould, the early morning light wincing through a gap in the curtains as though ashamed to be here.

And I'm not alone. My bedfellow – a woman, thank Christ – remains sound asleep (or unconscious), her small, trout-like face puckered up against my left shoulder. She's not much of a looker, but then it's been a while since I woke up next to one of those. Been a while since I woke up next to *anybody*, come to that.

The woman's forehead twitches. This high-pitched whining sound escaping from my mouth; I'd better stop. Don't want her waking, not until I can work out who/where/why I am. Diving face-first into the stale swamp of my pillow I muffle my wails until my vocal chords cease their phlegmy jangling.

Ouch. Though my dream's long-fled the punches continue. Feels like my brain wants out of my head in all directions, at once. Feels like my brain is screaming for its lawyer. It's worse at the back, near the crown, as if the poor thing is scrabbling on jellied hands and knees away from my nostrils, slapping against the back wall of my skull and yelling to be let out.

And I'm beginning to understand why. Through the hammering of my hangover and my snot-stuck nostrils and the sweat of the pillow and the aching wreckage of it all something is stinking *bad*.

Animal bad. Zoo bad.

Louise – my daughter – used to love watching the orangutans frowning out through the glass at us when she was a toddler, and for a bittersweet moment I'm back at Durrell – coddled by the stench – forcing a smile through the glass at the long armed non-men whilst simultaneously gagging on the smell of rotten fruit and scattered ape-waste entirely comparable to the one I'm getting now.

The past skims across surface of the present. Louise looks up at me with those blue doll eyes of hers, bringing fresh tears to my own.

Daddy can I..?

Not now. Up onto my elbows, the stink hitting me like a knee to the jaw. I gag, hand to mouth, the movement making my brain kick harder at its cage. The skin of my face is slick, greasy, like kebab meat; my palm comes away glistening.

The tiny bedroom swims into focus. There's excrement all over the bed, that top shelf orange stuff usually reserved for real connoisseurs, the terminally ill, the gastrically inflicted, chronic imbibers of liquids devastating to body and mind (tick). The sort of excrement that dissolves mere mortals from the inside out. You don't produce this stuff normally; it's got to be *ordered*.

Now a vertical stripe of the stuff separates me from this unknown woman who somehow – God alone knows how – sleeps on. Hauling myself up I attempt to identify the offending orifice. Of course the sludge is mine but I check anyway, drawn like some weird ghoul into a brief game of faecal dot-the-dot.

One spot, two spot, smear. My thighs are gummed with the stuff.

Case closed. Eat your heart out, Morse.

Other details: at some point in the night we've kicked off

the duvet, which now lies in a heap at the foot of the bed. A plug-in radiator regards me from the far wall like some disapproving droid from a low budget Sci-Fi movie. *You don't remember last night, do you?* it communicates in a harsh, dry heat. No, I don't.

The hangover's a composite; red wine, certainly, whiskey, Cognac perhaps, possibly even something more exotic. The razor-like edge to my headache and lingering chemical tang suggests a significant lager base. Stella, probably. A devastating combo whatever, to have uncaged my bowels like this. Third slick in a week; a new personal best.

My memory bag is empty, though trace impressions cling like fluff; lunch on a terrace somewhere, a fat man with a folder, falling heavily from a bus. Other than these my last real solid hat-hangable memories are of coming round on the floor of my flat yesterday morning (in a roughly comparable state) and cracking open the emergency Smirnoff. After that….

Slithering from the crime scene I kneel naked on the carpet, my forehead pressed against the mattress edge, tongue lolling like a gallowed corpse. Gazing down the pale canopy of my chest I spy an unfilled condom still in place and waving sadly at me like a tiny lost ghost. Things got that far, did they?

The woman mutters something in her sleep before rolling over on to her side of the bed, one arm now laid over her eyes in an expression of theatrical woe, her breasts spread flat like dropped blancmange.

I clamber to my feet. The bedroom's a sparse affair; cheap wardrobe, cheap dresser, a few photographs tacked to the wall, a spill of paperbacks on a shelf. Some of the spines bear an East

European script; Polish, Romanian, something like that.

I tiptoe shakily across the worn bedroom carpet and out onto an equally worn landing. The décor is unremittingly shabby. Most likely the girl's being carved up by one of the island's rent-butchers and hasn't the funds, inclination or spirit to do anything other than survive.

There's a bathroom at the top of the stairs, its grey, sad wallpaper peeling with mould. Above the toilet is a tiny framed print of the Scared Heart. The mould's got to baby Jesus too.

Opposite is a tiny bath with a cheap plastic shower attachment suckered over the tap. I clamber in. Turning the knobs I flick its weeping nozzle over my thighs and belly, start loosening the crusted orange mess with my right hand, Indian-style. Or do they use the left? Doesn't seem especially important right now. I'll Google it later.

My bladder's screaming. I let go whilst the water's still flowing, forgetting about the condom. Lacking the will and strength to slam the sluices I stare helplessly down at my expanding udder until it explodes, showering my groin and legs in wet yellow warmth.

Louise is laughing in my ear. *Water bombs daddy! Let's make water bombs!* She loved them, my daughter, loved anything to do with water. I remember us trying to pelt our neighbour's cat from the first floor window of our house, back when we still had one. Louise's mother didn't like it, said I was surreptitiously promoting war, but then she'd be the one to know about that. She'd know all about war.

I wonder if there's any water balloon action going on in that new flat of theirs. Probably not; my ex-wife was never any fun. I console myself by hurling an imagined condom full of frothy orange piss at her head (most likely soaking someone innocent and needy instead, some hypothetical bystander, some kid in a wheelchair, some suited old gent on his way to a friend's funeral. What is it the kids say? *Cos that's how I roll*).

I've showered the last of the *shiss* from my ankles now. Cleansed (in the very loosest sense of the word) I clamber weakly from the bath tub and spend a minute gulping water from the tap before scraping myself dry with a small towel the texture of toast.

Time to address those bed sheets. Next to the bath is a set of shaky plastic drawers, and in the second of these I find some disposable razors. Crushing one of these against the laminate floor with a tub of moisturiser I grind the plastic frame with my makeshift mortar until the blade breaks free. That'll do.

Back in the bedroom Sleeping Not-so-Beauty remains unconscious. Better still, she's rolled over on to her left side, leaving a few more inches of unsullied white bed sheet between her and my shame.

Her movement has also revealed a badly inked tattoo of my face on her left buttock. The scar on the left cheek, the broad forehead, the rough curls. Definitely me. A crudely drawn speech bubble curls off down her thigh. Inside this, the letters S H A H.

Whatever. I move quickly, silently, working the razor down the length of the bed sheet, my eyes fixed nervously on the rise and fall of her back, breath held against the hot roar of my filth. At one point the woman stirs, causing me to freeze, yet this is only to scratch the face – *my* face – on her backside.

Eventually I succeed in shearing my half of the bed sheet away from hers. Having carefully rolled it up into a nasty little bundle I step out on to the landing, loitering with my foul package like some kind of anti-Father Christmas. *Here you go, kid; enjoy.*

Now what? There's a small window open at the top of the stairs. Maybe I'll just throw it out of that. I could do with knowing where I am on the island, and a trip to the window will see two birds killed with one soiled fabric stone.

A peek out the window confirms my suspicions. St Helier. Early morning. Somewhere near the shabbier end of town, if the beige three story houses, corroded railings and residents' parking bays opposite me are anything to go by. Some guy in overalls is opening up the Costcutter on the corner, but other than that the street is empty.

Saturday? Possibly. Names of days don't seem to matter as much of late.

Have it, St Helier. Having tugged open the window I shove the soiled bundle through, letting it drop to the pavement below. Not a good time to be walking by, though the worst part of me hopes that someone innocent and needy is. Failing that, my ex-neighbour's cat would do just fine.

Job done on the job done. I take a deep breath, peering down the staircase at the sparse wood-floored hallway below. The front door's visible, though I won't be creeping down just yet. Keen as I am to be clear of this shabby hole – preferably in my clothes – I've a hunch that I'm on a case. A little detail would be nice. We private investigators thrive on them.

Creeping back to the bedroom I slither back into the bed,

grimacing down onto the bare mattress, wincing as my limbs and head protest. Keeping my back to the girl I reach down for the duvet and I pull it up over our lower torsos sufficiently to hide my razor-work.

It's as I'm doing this that the woman stirs, extending an exploratory hand, the palm of which falls flat upon my upturned left hip.

'Brian.'

I freeze. Blind dates have never been my thing, especially ones kicking off in cack-smeared beds. And what's with the Brian? That's not my name, not by a long shot.

'Brian,' she croaks again, the sharp tips of her nails pressing slowly into my flesh. 'You been a bad boy, Brian. You been a real bad boy.'

2 – Pillow Talk

Brian. Hardly the most spectacular of names. Carries with it the vague promise of intelligence, a kind of hard boiled nerdiness suggestive of quiet men in lab coats, software programmers still living with their mum. Must be embarrassing being a Brian and stupid with it, though I'm guessing the irony would pass said Brian by. It takes a certain degree of intelligence to spot that you've been dished an inappropriate first name. Marigold, for instance.

The only actual Brian I ever knew was a baggy-jowled geek that used to mooch around my school looking glum. Real passive aggressive sort, ran a good line in telephone bomb scares until he got expelled. I remember him making me cry one during one of our school Sports Days, back when I was chubby and innocent and sweet, before booze and loss chewed the flesh from my bones. The final scores were up and our house had beaten his, the stadium's speaker system blaring this fact to the assembled throng. I'd made the mistake of cheering.

'No thanks to you, fatty,' Brian had snarled, making all the kids around us laugh. Spoiled my day entirely. Though Brian did have a point; I *had* come last in all of my races.

My humiliation back then was a sign of things to come, perhaps. I can still hear my friends' laughter now. Funny how the little hurts linger in spite of the large, like the tiny scars still itching on your blown-off leg.

'Hey. You there?' The woman gives my buttock a slap.

'Morning,' I grunt.

My bedfellow rustles around behind me as I remain motionless, face to the door. I'm not ready to do the whole face to face thing yet. Not keen on intimacy. I find it spoils things.

'Christ! What's that smell?'

I really should have opened the bedroom window. Though I've become inured to it by now (either that or my nasal receptors have simply disintegrated) the air is clearly still laced with the hot tang of my filth.

'Your dog?'

'I don't have a bloody dog.'

'You sure?'

'How many times? No dog.'

East European, certainly. Voice a harsh mid-range, needle already flicking amber on the bullshit gauge.

'Turn around, Brian.'

Brian again. Then it hits me.

Of course. This old trick. The fake name's a memo left for my future self, a signal mnemonic deployed for the assistance of post-binge, *après*-blackout recall. There's bound to be other clues round here, other crumbs dropped by my inebriate self if I can work out where to look.

B for Brian, then. It's all about that first letter, this system – if I regain consciousness as a Mark, Michael or Monty then I'm on a Missing Persons job. For Elijah, Earnest or Elvis (yes it happened; I was in a real bad way) read Extortion. Aaron for Adultery. And so on.

Blackmail it is, then. I'm working a blackmail case. Perhaps.

'Turn around. Show me your face.'

'Do I have to?'

Faces. Never been a huge fan of mine. The big Roman nose, those saggy eye-bags, that extra helping of chin. I've often thought that my grid resembles an amateur portrait of some ugly guy pretending to be me, and never did understand what Louise's mother saw in it to love. The leaving part I can understand, the screaming and the suing and the lawyers I get, it's just the four years of actual marriage that have me stumped. Four years of staring into this thing. Why do that to yourself? Unless she was sick of course, some kind of messed up self-reviling masochist, in which case I guess I'm lucky to be rid of her.

'Turn around.'

I roll over into the sour heat of the girl's breath. She's prettier now she's awake, though there's still something mildly amphibious about her thin head and that permanent pout. Her eyes are as dark as her hair, and twinkle mischievously as they roam my face. Late twenties, I'm guessing.

'Seen worse,' she says, after a moment's genuine consideration. 'You smoke?'

'Of course.' There's a moment of awkward silence as we shuffle apart and up into sitting posture. A packet of cigarettes gets offered. I take one, lowering its tip into the flame of her lighter. Together we face forward in awkward parallel, sucking and blowing into the messed air.

'You have a drawing of my face on your buttock. I'm touched.'

'Ha!' She rolls her eyes. '*I'm* the one that was fucking touched. You did last night with biro.'

'Right.'

'Is no worry. Like I said; for two hundred pounds you can do whatever you like. Except anal.'

'Two hundred pounds.'

'Two hundred pounds.'

'But no anal.'

'No anal.'

We smoke on a little more, the air before us roiling thick and blue. My stomach lets out a long and audible gurgle. The girl snorts something meaty, swallows.

'So I paid you two hundred pounds.'

'Not yet. You *will*.'

What was the euphemism good old Dr Griffiths used to use? Our family doctor always had a way with words. *Unpredictable social outcomes.* That was it. *Insistent abuse of alcohol combined with sporadic ingestion of anti-depressants can lead to unpredictable social outcomes.* Duloxetine on the rocks, Venlafaxine and coke, four pints of serotonin-norepinephrene reuptake inhibitor and lime; dice-rolling, essentially. And plump old Dr Griffiths was right, if by *unpredictable social outcomes* he meant running naked round supermarkets, writing long, astonishingly coherent letters to the BBC about the decline in broadcast quality since the demise of *Last of the Summer Wine*, stuffing bread into post boxes, impulsive buying of flowers for the handicapped, urinating against walls and doors, confessing on buses to the assassination of Seattle-based grunge guitarists, professing to the reading of auras, proposing to shoes, pretending to be a private detective etc etc, all of which are part of my ever-growing repertoire, half of which I don't remember doing, the other half of which I consume alcohol and pills to forget. Call it a hobby. It keeps me out of trouble, at the very least.

Prostitutes, though? Never. Although yes, the Booze-Til-It-Goes-Black!™ board has hundreds of segments, and yes, the spinner can land on any one, so hey, maybe I just did. Maybe my libido staged an unexpected resurrection last night, punching a fist up through the clod and grabbing the nearest fish-faced skeleton it could find.

'You remember anything from last night?'

'Bits,' I lie. 'A vague outline. Parts.'

'Such as?'

Snow White sighs. Reaching over to the bedside table she crushes her fag into the large glass ashtray balanced atop a ruffled copy of Coelho's *The Alchemist*. Then she throws off the covers, gets to her feet and starts rummaging round on the floor for some pants and a bra. I watch her scrawny nakedness out of the corner of my eye, noting the days-old yellow bruising beneath her clavicle.

'You turn up at hotel bar around half eight.' She speaks quickly whilst sliding a pair of black knickers up over her hips. 'You drink pints at the bar whilst asking me all sort of questions. Questions, questions, questions. About bloody dogs. You want to know if I've seen any dogs recently. If I know anyone in hotel with bloody Labrador dog. I say no. You ask how long I've been working here. You ask me a whole load of stuff while you drink all your pints.'

I study the cigarette smouldering between my fingers. Regal. Cheap and nasty, like sucking on burning woodchip. Perhaps if I keep dragging on it in like this the right neuron's going to fire, setting off a firecracker chain of recollections. Or perhaps I'll just be sick.

Turning her back to me the girl bends down to the floor, causing the biro portrait on her lower buttock to raise its eyebrows in mute query.

'Someone you know comes into the bar. Old man with big white beard like Father Christmas. He buys red wine and you drink it with him, leave me alone for a bit, thank the God I'm saying. Then he goes and you come back asking about bloody dogs again. Then you offer me two hundred pounds to have sex with you.'

'And Father Christmas? Where did he go?'

'I don't know. Back to bloody North Pole I guess. Two hundred bloody pounds you say,' she says, scooping her breasts up into her bra. 'We agreed.'

'Which hotel are we talking about here?'

She turns to me with a face like a thumped haddock. '*What?* You don't even remember what hotel you were in? What are you, bloody crazy?'

'Was it the Ambassadeur?'

'Of course the bloody Ambassadeur.'

The Ambassadeur. Well that's something. Recollections of my arrival there bob like torch-lit corpses on a dark and choppy sea. Stumbling down the bus steps and into a chill wind. The spray of seawater over the sea wall. A smash of glass on pavement. The rain slick in orange pools across the coast road, the lurching lights of the approaching hotel.

'And right now we're in St Helier.'

'No shit, Sherwood.'

'Sherlock.'

'Sherlock. Whatever. You fall over in the toilets, I help you up, we get a cab back here. We try have sex but your dick no work. Then you fall asleep.' She barks all of this at me whilst pulling on some grey jogging bottoms and a hooded top.

The Hotel Ambassadeur. Family run three star on the southeast coast of the island, a ten minute drive from town. A class below the island's finest hotels yet popular enough. Got a nice little residents' bar, couple of mid-range function rooms. I seem to recall an office party there a few years back, before I took a liquid machete to it all.

Santa's most probably my old friend Babs Le Gros. Babs lives at La Rocque, a little further east. Haven't seen him for a good few months. Is this latest encounter down to business or sheer chance? I'll call him later, see if he can fill me in.

'Get up, please. Two hundred pounds, you said.'

'That's not going to happen.' I climb woozily to my feet. 'Apologies for this, by the way.' I gesture at my nakedness, start kicking at the assorted mess of garments on the floor in an attempt to find my trousers. My trench coat's hanging from that chair over there. One shoe over by that wall. Location of underpants unknown.

'Then I go to the fucking police.' She spins, suddenly angry, chin jutting. 'I go to fucking Immigration and tell your boss you offered me two hundred to suck your maggot there and then beat me up and refused to pay.'

'*Immigration?*'

'It's where you work, dick head? It's why you ask all those bloody questions last night, yes? And look. This.' She pinches a flap of the yellowed skin beneath her throat. 'You did this with bloody knee. Trying to feed me maggot. I tell them that. I tell your bloody boss.'

'My *boss*?'

'What are you, fucking parrot? Your boss. You Immigration inspector, right?'

Wrong, though I can see why she'd be worried if this were truly the case. At only nine miles by five and bearing close to a hundred thousand souls Jersey's rag-tag local government has been cracking down on low-paid illegal workers of late, with those lacking the requisite work permits being melted down and sold as mansion wax to the tax-shy foreign elite. I'm guessing my friend here is one of the former.

'Now listen,' I say, my attempted cool instantly undone by the kiss of exposed testicles against inner thigh. 'Despite what I may or may not have told you last night – because I really can't recall either way – I'm certainly *not* an Immigration...'

The girl starts hammering on the floor with the ball of her foot. *Bang bang bang.*

'...I'm more of a...*freelance fact-gatherer*, if you will. Speaking of which I was wondering...'

Bangbangbang.

'...if perhaps we could just take a step back and...'

A door creaks opens downstairs. My words trail off at the sound of fast and heavy stomping on the stairs. Here comes the cavalry. I spin round in search of a suitable fig leaf, succeeding only in inducing a wave of nausea that dumps me buttocks-down on the bed.

Thumping on the landing. Mixed grunts. I look up as a two-headed monster rears into view, filling the doorway.

'Putain de merde, Franck,' it snarls. 'Regardez cette!'

Each of the monster's heads has a separate body, one of which steps forward into the room. Swallowing hard I stare up at an approaching six-foot-something skinhead with a face like sculptured spam and a barbed-wire tattoo around his throat. His thick woollen jumper is frayed at the cuffs; his grey jeans are dirty and still damp at the knees. Behind him the second body peers on tiptoes over the partner's shoulder, his thin, toothy face crinkled in a ratty sneer, his head equally devoid of anything remotely worth a ruffle. He's wearing a black bomber jacket and camouflage pants.

Both men are wearing Doc Martins; both have clumps of wet soil and grass mashed into the seams. About them the air sizzles with criminality. *French* criminality at that.

'Morning, gents.' I give them a little wave, whilst calculating my chances of surviving a head-first dive through the bedroom window. Easy: glass + gravity + pavement = n, n being 'the hospital.'

'J'ai vu plus d'un infant,' says the big guy, gesturing at my groin. 'Vous etes malades? Et quelle est cette odour? Yola?' He swats the air beneath his nose with grazed knuckles, nose wrinkling, his mouth sharpening into a shocked zero of disgust.

Yola shrugs, though is beginning to take a closer interest in my side of the bed, where shorn sheets and the furthest reaches of a vague yet unmistakably brown constellation are now clearly visible.

'Tu est homesicky, yes?' I smile, pointing into the fouled air.

'We give you fucking *homesick*,' shouts the little rat-faced fellow, trying to wriggle through the gap between his meathead accomplice and the doorframe. 'Andre! *Deplacer!*'

But Andre doesn't move. As Franck squirms behind him he slowly folds his arms, watching Yola with obvious distaste as she scurries round the bed towards him.

'Two hundred, you said!' Yola snarls at the men. 'Give me my money. Here he is. I did what you...'

'Stop!' snarls Andre, lashing out with the back of his hand. 'Vous receverez votre argent rapidement!'

Yola retreats, scowling. Franck has squeezed into the room and is rummaging through my jacket, pulling various pieces of expired plastic and faded receipts from its pockets.

'OK. You come wiz us now,' says Andre darkly, gesturing at me to rise.

'But I haven't even had breakfast. Some *croissants*, surely.'

Andre gives this some thought. 'Il veut le petite-dejeuner' he calls over to Franck, who is now brandishing my debit card triumphantly, having located it in the pocket of my coat.

'Oui?' *Wah?* Franck shrugs.

'Oui. Pas de probleme, monsieur.' Andre clicks his fingers. 'Franck. Les pantalons. *Ici.*'

Franck throws over my chinos. In a blur of grey fabric Andre grabs the bottom of the legs and loops the crotch over my head. A sharp tug pulls me up on to my feet and up towards the descending wall of his forehead. There's a fairly hideous crunch as the bridge of my nose connects and then I'm back on the bed, clutching and stunned, blood pouring into the trembling chalice of my palms.

'Bon appétit, *putain*,' sniggers Franck.

'Allez!' roars Andre.

Rough hands grip my shoulders. Yola is shouting something about her money, about the blood and the shit on her bed. I'm hoisted from the floor and dragged painfully down the staircase, face buried deep in the dark woollen musk of Andre's armpit, elbow twisted hard behind my back, the back of my throat filling with warm rusty gunk.

Not the best of starts, this. In fact as far as Worst Mornings Ever go this one's definitely up there in the top eighty-five.

The front door opens. Cold air bites. I'm dragged down the pavement for a few metres before being tipped forwards into an open car boot, landing heavily on my elbows. Someone hurls my legs in after me, followed by a little rag of damp cloth that settles on my face. I wait for the lid of the boot to slam and total darkness to descend before reaching up and pressing the rag to my nose.

Of course. They've given me back my underpants.

So you see it's not *all* bad.

3 – Things Take a Dive

Had these real big teeth, did Babs Le Gros. Bugs, we used to call him. I can still picture those central incisors of his, twin squares of white in the shadows of the stands. It was easy enough to clamber over the wall into Springfield stadium and on certain nights we'd do just that, smashing down bottles of cheap cider or smuggled spirits until one by one we puked, cried or collapsed. *Mummy*, Babs had howled one time from the mud of the goalmouth; *mummy come take me home.* Big white petals, those teeth of his, alternatively there then not-there in the moonlight as the length of Babs' bottle rose and fell.

Those glorious mid-teen years were the start of it all. Saturday nights we drank like ninjas, gathering in the cold to sow the seeds of our respective downfalls, tramping them down into our souls' earth with bone-white Reeboks, watering freely with sickly pish. Merrydown. Strongbow. 20/20. Diamond White. Even now I can recall the bracing sharpness of the evening's opening glug, the winter air gnawing at our fingertips and faces as we chased inebriation like daft puppies after our favourite ball.

Babs and I lost touch shortly after sixth form, and so it was with genuine and unexpected pleasure that I found myself sharing a corridor with him at Wallace Lodge (a sympathetic magistrate having awarded me an eight week residential stay) some thirty-odd years later.

Mr Booze had not been kind to Bugs. Those glorious front teeth were gone, for starters, the conversion awarded, accepted and skilfully buried in the back of his head several years back by some jobsworthy doorman. His eyes had all but shrunken into the ragged craters of his face. Eczema ravaged his hairless scalp. Somewhere along the way he'd acquired a limp. The beard was new though – we liked the beard – and made sure to tell him so, if ever we caught him looking glum, which was always.

'I lost it all,' Babs had blubbed to the circle during one of our group sessions. Babs usually resisted The Blub – unlike myself, for whom a gentle and incessant weeping had become the norm – so the sudden wet crumpling of his face had taken us all by surprise.

'I lost it all,' he'd whined. 'And for what? For *what*? My children hate me, my ex-wife refuses to even pick up the phone, my own *brother* moved to Alderney without letting me know. *Alderney*, for Christ's sake! I've no money, no job, and no friends. My hands shake so bad I can barely hold a pen. The doctor tells me its only a matter of time until sclerosis kicks in, and then...'

'*Cirr*hosis,' I'd corrected, drawing a scowl from Felicity, our 'facilitator'. 'Sclerosis is when your muscle hardens. Totally different thing.'

Ah, Wallace Lodge, where are you now? The mind-flaying order of it all; those sad, wilting pot plants; that brutal pastel décor; the ever-patient staff; the TV room with its boxed sets of dreary eighties' detective shows. A hell of sorts, though I've no shame in admitting that at times I miss it.

I'm missing it right now, in fact. But then one tends to miss a lot of things when you're locked in the boot of some hooligans' car. The make's unspecified. Red, I think, if that's any use. I did catch a glimpse before the boot lid came down though it was all over rather quickly, the being dragged and beaten and lifted and dumped into this fuzzy little darkness bit. A few bursts of prime French invective, a bullet of warm Gallic flob to the back of my head and then on to the uncomfortable memory-lit blackness in which I'm lying now, bumping along on my back, an uneventful journey broken only by the awkward reapplication of my underpants. Well, a man's got to keep his dignity.

The dark I can bear, but this thirst has become intolerable. I reach around, finding a plastic bottle of something or other at the bottom of a soggy cardboard box. De-icing fluid from the smell of it. Disappointing. Desperate for moisture I swill a mouthful of the stuff regardless, being careful not to swallow too much. The cool liquid is harsh and oddly sweet but I've gargled worse.

As well as the bottle I find some flexible cable and what I'm guessing from the fuzz and squeeze to be a tennis ball. All rather handy should I be called upon to entertain a small child, though hardly the stuff from which to fashion an *A-Team* style break out.

The de-icing fluid is making my head swim in a not wholly unpleasant way. I take another small sip, re-screw the cap and lie back in my automotive coffin like Everyman in his underpants (*Next*, white Y-Front, pack of three at a perfectly reasonable £6.99) hurtling blindly towards my uncertain fate like every other human being on this sorry spinning rock, caged to the pore by the impenetrable and pressing blackness, blithe of purpose and already disintegrating, skin, organs, bones and face searing in slow-motion hysteria towards the eradicating scorch of oblivion.

Worse, I need a piss. Rolling over on to my side I coax my slug free of its elastic cage and jet hot revenge into the corner of the boot. I spit a little too, summoning what little sickly moisture there is in my mouth into a little rope of unwinding drool. *Have it, you French swine.* If nothing else I've cost them a valet.

The minutes grind by. My bruises accrue. Eventually we pull to a stop, wheels grinding over what I take to be gravel. The boot door clunks open. I ask if we're there yet whilst squinting up into the blinding white. A cold rain spits through the space between the craned heads of my two French kidnappers; Andre staring down at me with all the affection of a man who's just spied blood in his stool, Franck shaking his ratty little head in revulsion. He's chewing gum. I want some.

'Allez.'

Andre reaches down, all snarls and body odour. Strong fingers grip. I'm hoisted out of the boot by the shoulders, dragged across what is indeed gravel and thrown to the ground, my bare flesh registering a fright of spiky cold.

'Up.'

I clamber shivering to my knees. We're in a car park on an exposed section of the island's north coast, up near Sorel Point. My chariot – a battered red Renault – is the only vehicle present. Beyond this gravel circle, off past the main road from which we've just pulled in there is little else but low fields, bushes, a line of telephone masts disappearing into the mist. Seawards at the car-park's edge the land falls abruptly away into an east-west stretch of rugged furze-topped cliffs, their chests bared to the foamed fists of the English Channel, waves chopping and roaring at the rocks below. Wheeling seagulls screech above a nettle-edged drop.

Teeth clattering I hug myself in an attempt to shield my bare skin from the chill northerly wind. Pointless. The gusting sea air is icy, unforgiving. I wonder how far up my torso I can stretch these underpants.

No time to find out. No sooner have I reached for the elastic then I'm yanked up by the armpit and shoved into the sparse thicket adjoining the car park. My legs falter. Andre shoves me roughly in the back. Stone shards and brambles compete to tear at the soles of my feet as we descend a narrow and barely beaten dirt track.

I'm wearing long-johns from now on. To Hell with fashion.

'Anyone f...f...fancy a p...p...pint?'

'Ta bouche!'

'There's a l...lovely pub not f...f...far from...'

The jab comes quickly, just below my ribcage, left side. Winded, I drop to all fours, Nature's carpet pressing in sharp and hard against my kneecaps and palms.

Fingers in my hair. Head yanked back. Ugly French guy in my face.

'You stop talking, *putain*,' snarls Andre. 'Is talking get you into this troubles, yes? You asking Yola too many questions.'

Dr Griffiths, I whisper. *I demand to see Dr Griffiths*, but we're back on our way now, Andre dragging me down a bramble-lined mud path running roughly parallel with the cliff edge. To our left the land tumbles away in a series of bushy inclines and sheer drops, at the base of which a gunmetal sea barrels and writhes around islands of jagged rock.

Out over the Channel the sky has collapsed into the horizon, its line hidden behind a thick shroud of grey. On a clear day you can see the coast of France from here. Mercifully today is not one of those days.

'Andre!' calls Franck, from behind. 'Vous pouvez le voir a partir d'ici!'

'Ta guelle, canule!'

Irritated, Andre gives me a shove, pushing me off the gravel path and up through the bushes towards a spur of rock that pokes out over the cliff edge. Shuddering with cold I'm made to walk the granite plank, shuffling up its slow rise until I'm nearing the edge. It's not quite a sheer drop from here, though I'm none too keen on the rocky bounce and tumble should I fall. Down at the base of the cliff the sea bears its jagged fangs, hissing like a wild wet beast.

'Maybe this teach you not to play detective, Monsieur Dark,' says Andre, leaning in close behind me. 'Now. Any last requests?'

'Yes. M...mouthwash. Your b...breath smells like an elephant's b...balls.'

And that's just for starters, I want to add. I'd also like the last seven years of my life erased from whatever abstract meta-records the universe holds. Every molecule brushed or in some way affected by my existence during this time – I want them all got rid of, smashed one by one at CERN until nothing remains of them but the space occasioned by their absence.

Then I'd like to start again.

Fatherhood; I'll get it right this time. Zap me right back to the night of Louise's conception, if you would. Her mother and I sprawled naked on our hotel bed in Rome. The empty bottles of wine. The distant Vatican peeping balefully in through the window as I fiddle with my condom, the nick through which my daughter will elbow her way into this life already unknowingly in place.

Sod it; I won't even bother with the Durex this time. *We're going to have a daughter anyway*, I'll tell Louise's soon-to-be-mother. *Condom or not. So let's just go for it, yes? Keep that old Pope of yours happy.* And out the corner of my eye I'll see the Vatican raising a gigantic white thumbs-up and know that finally God is on my side, finally God is...

A violent gust of wind slaps me back to reality, needling my upper body and forcing me back a step into Andre's outstretched palms. The seagulls have picked up their squawking; *come on, come on, come on*.

Another push. Forward I go, arms wrapped around my torso, shivering. A few more feet and I'm going over. Not much of this ledge left.

I squint about for some kind of human assistance, finding none. Too early in the morning for cliff walkers. Something catches my eye atop a chunk of cliff a few hundred metres to my right. Some sort of half-arsed Martello Tower, its one visible window staring across the gulf at me, the discoloured brick arch above it an eyebrow, raised and sympathetically aghast. I get the odd feeling that it's trying to tell me something.

'Move!' shouts Andre behind me. I close my eyes, fleeing somewhere warmer, somewhere with bed sheets and wine, waving back at the Vatican and wondering what the Pope would do if stripped to his papal underpants and rendered a holy blur of shivering flesh about to be pushed into the sea. Would he bless his assailants, thanking the Lord Almighty for the cliff from which he was about to be thrown? Would the papal pants be boxers or briefs? Or something else altogether, something more in keeping with his role as official representative of the Almighty? How best ensure the continued hygiene and good condition of the closest thing to God's anus on earth?

Louise's mother would be the one to ask. She's spent a lifetime kissing it, after all. Perhaps I'll try phoning her again when all this is over. Open with the Pope question, move on to the usual business of begging her to let me see my daughter.

'*Quoi?*' shouts Andre, through the wind and the smashing of the waves below. 'Why you laughing? What's so funny?'

'N...nothing,' I manage, toes curling over the edge of the rock, eyes to the sky. Because let's face it; nothing really is. And this isn't laughter anyway, this shuddering, this noise coming out of my mouth. That isn't *rain* rolling down my cheeks.

Daddy can I..?

'Give my love to ze crabs.'

The sea and the sky and everything else dissolves as Andre gives me final push forwards. My hands clutch for railings that were never there. My feet scramble but the rock just ran out. Then it's just air, and space, and the drop.

4 – Non-Attack of the Half Naked Cyborg Assassin

About that last request thing.

I've got two more.

One, I'd like to know what on earth dragged me out to the Hotel Ambassadeur last night. And two, I'd like a ladder. Not a huge one; a step ladder would do, one of those little ones you somehow unfold to replace the angel on top of the Christmas tree having kicked the whole thing down in a drunken rage one Christmas Eve in front of your sobbing wife and child – one of those. Just to get me up off this rainy ledge. Just to kick-start the process of hauling myself home.

To the flat, I should say. Home's long gone for me.

I'm guessing that Laurel *et* Hardy have carried out similar mock-executions at this spot before. Not a bad effort, to be fair. Had me fooled, right up until that outstretched palm of brambles and branches caught me mid-fall and rolled me backwards on to this little rocky shelf where I'm shivering now. That last minute spin to the left; Andre knew what he was doing. Death was never part of the plan. This was a warning, an invitation to stay away. From what, though? Yola? All this to protect some hotel worker from getting her wrist slapped over some missing hypothetical work permit? Hardly.

Why the scare tactics then? For whose benefit? There are plenty out there who wish me ill – and not *all* of them ex-friends and family – though none I can think of that would resort to so elaborate a charade.

Has to be something with this case I'm on, this latest

detective 'episode' as Dr Griffiths would no doubt call it. If only I could remember *what* that something was. Or *whom*. Or *why*.

The shock of my non-fall has whiplashed a few more details into my brain – a vague memory of being summoned from the bath tub (in which I was lying *sans* water and fully clothed) by a phone call yesterday morning, time spent shouting at a fat man, and that tower...that tower over there... though of course this may all just be something I've read, or watched, or drunk.

It'll come. For now I'd best get off this cliff face. Reaching upwards I drive my numbed fingers into the earth, searching for a suitable handhold. Weeds pull free, showering me in soil. Small rocks loosen and tumble, striking me on the shoulders and chest. I clout my knee, mash my forehead in some nettles. Eventually I am able to grab a handle and haul myself up, digging my bare feet into the rock face and scraping my belly over the rough, brambled brow.

Having regained *terra firma* I trudge back up the dirt track to the car park. All that's left of my mock executioners are twin gashes in the wet gravel where the tyres of their car have spun and cut. They've gone, taking all hopes of clothes, jacket, and wallet with them.

Not so my Nokia, however, which I spy lying on the grass. The wet's killed it but a slow, numb-fingered fumble finds the SIM card present and intact. Left for me or accidentally dropped? Who knows, though hopefully there's something on it that will help me work out what I've been up to these past twenty-four hours.

The rain has thickened. Head bowed, arms wrapped around me as though bound by an invisible straightjacket I trudge off along the road. Cold, effort and adrenalin have erased all trace of this morning's hangover, leaving me floundering in an absolute anguish of sobriety. The effects of the de-icing fluid have worn off and now those stubborn neurons of mine are sparking again, spanning gaps, rebuilding bridges. Out from these come stumbling the trolls of memory, clubs in hand, blinking in the sober light, already grinning at the violence to come. They'll need chasing back under, and soon.

Heavy spirits call for heavy spirits. Where's the nearest pub? There's nothing within eyeshot save the dark crescent of the road, the deep, dripping foliage on either side, a hint of houses lurking far off beyond the mist.

I've a long trek back to town. A shame I hadn't seen this coming and set up a sponsorship form. Could have raised some funds to pay off the thousands I'm supposed to owe to Wallace Lodge. Made a phone call to the Guinness Book of Records, even, taken a decent swing at the record for Longest Walk Ever Undertaken by a Forty-Three Year Old Alcoholic in Nothing but his Underpants in the Rain.

I make it a quarter mile down the road when I catch the approaching chug of a car engine from the curve up ahead. Here's my chance. Working on the assumption that I'm currently at the lower end of the Feasible Hitch-hiker spectrum I drop to the grass, raising my scuffed-white knees for increased visibility. No way they'll miss this man-sized Caesar salad by the side of the road.

Sure enough I hear the car engine slowing even as it gets louder. Sounds like a big one. Diesel. My money's on a Land Rover.

Tyres crunch, closer, stop.

A car door clicks open.

'My God!' Female voice. Thirty-something. Sharp, bossy edge. 'Dan! Quickly...call the police or something. Ambulance. Both. Oh bloody hell just look at him.'

Another door clicks open. Heavy footsteps slapping my way.

'Oh fucking hell Dan. Is he...is..?'

'Help.' I roll over on to my side, extending a trembling hand towards my rescuers. Framed by the mountainous black Land Rover (told you) is an elfin, pony-tailed blond in her late thirties. She's decked pretty much as you'd expect a woman emerging from a mountainous black Land Rover to be; glittery cashmere pullover, bright white jeans, fur-lined knee length boots. Her face is handsome, if a little pinched around the brow. From around the front of the vehicle comes a large, wide-jawed man a few years older, his large tanned head perched above his North Face gilet like the seated ruler of some rich and well-fortified kingdom.

'Bloody hell mate. Are you alright?' He frowns down at me, hands on his hips.

'Does he *look* alright, Dan? Call the police!'

'Are you...are you hurt?' asks Dan.

'Just c...cold,' I stammer, attempting to clamber to my feet. 'I have these f...fits. Forget who I am. It's happened before. Don't worry. I'm s...safe. Just a bit confused.'

Which is the truth, of sorts.

'Blanket, darling. Boot of the car,' says Dan, kneeling down to help me up. He flinches a little as his fingers make contact with my flesh.

Julia stiffens, clearly repulsed at the sight of the white, underpant-clad mantis clinging to her husband and clearly less than enamoured at the whole Lazarus routine. She's paling beneath that tan of hers, I'm sure. Still, the ladies at lunch will have trouble beating this one and Facebook is going to go *wild*.

'Julia! Please, darling. The picnic rug. The poor chap's freezing.'

I eye Dan's body warmer with envy. Flung on no doubt with the remains of his low calorie high fibre diet still clinging to his teeth. Left pocket reassuringly weighed with an expensive wallet bearing all manner of high end plastic, loyalty cards, a wedge of ready cash. And beneath it all, under that expensive cardigan, a hairless chest, a six pack, a tiny set of wholesome balls shaved bare.

At knifepoint. By Julia.

'Looks like you've hurt your face as well. Shall we take you to the hospital?'

I nod, pathetically. Sounds like a plan. A+E are bound to have some old clothes kicking about (I've certainly donated a few over the years) and I can be back at the flat within minutes.

Julia returns from the Land Rover with a large red rug. I thank her, wasting no time in wrapping it tightly around me.

'From Caesar s...salad to chicken wrap.' My joke causes Julia's lips to tighten. She throws a concerned glance at Dan, who pretends not to notice as he escorts me back to the car.

'Jump in the back,' he says. 'That's Esmie by the way.'

A cabbage-faced teenager with ginger plaits pokes her head out of the lowered rear passenger window. Face crinkled as though recently smote with the Frying Pan of Disgust she's trying to ward me off Van Helsing-style with her iPhone.

'Esmie for God's sake,' snaps Julia. 'Put that away.'

Scowling, the girl retreats inside the belly of the metal beast, quickly scurrying up against the far door as Dan helps me up on to the back seat. Her iPhone – or rather its camera lens – remains locked on me the whole time.

'That's far enough, mister. You smell funny.'

'Esmie,' growls Dan, retaking the driver's seat. 'Did you not hear what Julia said?'

'Jesus, Dad. This is Snapchat *gold*,' slurps Esmie, her mouth a glistening mess of spit and metal braces. 'You just found a man lying in the road in his *underpants*.'

'Esmie!' Julia snaps with barely restrained fury as Dan pulls off. 'This poor man's ill and needs our help. Put that bloody phone away. Step-daughters,' she mutters, clearly eager to clarify that this ginger fruit is not of her loins. 'Who'd have them?'

'I'm a terminator,' I blurt.

The car stops suddenly, jolting both myself and Esmie forwards. There's an almost audible creak of leather as Dan's boot arches back off the accelerator. We sit there, unmoving.

Silence. Rain drums the windscreen. The wipers go *swoosh*.

'Like in the film,' I continue. '*Terminator*. Arnold Schwarzenegger starts off lying on a road in nothing but his underwear. I'm a bit like that, yes? Only I'm not Austrian. And I doubt I'll ever make Governor of California.'

'Right,' says Julia, urgently seeking Dan's eyes in the rear view mirror.

'Okay,' says Dan.

'So what you're basically saying,' says Esmie, after a

41

moment's silence, 'is that you're a cyborg assassin that's been sent back from the future to kill us all? *Sweet*. Well done Dad.' She reaches forward and pats Dan gently on the shoulder. 'Good move with the stopping and all that. Nice.'

'Um,' says Julia. 'You remember nothing about your personal circumstances, yet you can remember the start of *Terminator*?'

'It's a good film.'

'It is, actually,' nods Dan, seemingly satisfied that at no point do I plan to rip apart the vehicle with my bear hands and slaughter them all. He pulls off again, the Land Rover accelerating out into the road. 'Second one too. Then they got rubbish. Often the way.'

Esmie rolls her eyes.

'I can see you're going for the same look,' I tell her, rubbing my index finger across the front of my teeth. 'Skynet starts here.'

'Jesus, Dad! Did you hear that?'

'The man's just joking, dear,' murmurs Dan, with a sideways glance at Julia, who can't resist a smile.

Esmie blushes and closes her mouth. She doesn't say much for a while after that. On we roll.

'These fits only affect a certain portion of my brain,' I explain, warmed a little as we head south towards St Helier, houses gathering like fluff. 'They're like localised electrical storms. I can still remember a load of stuff. It's just the personal details that get scrambled.'

And that really is the truth. I *do* get these electrical

brainstorms that scramble the things closest to me. Only there's a proper term for it – *manic depression* – and the details that get scrambled are generally my relationships with other people; work colleagues, wives, daughters, people like that. And memories *are* a problem for me, which is why I spend my days drinking to get rid of them.

'Thanks for this, by the way,' I say, waggling the hip-flask up towards the front. 'Just what my doctor would order, if I could remember who he was.'

Vodka. And I hadn't even had to ask. Not enough to get truly groovy on, but enough to wash those trolls back under their bridge for a while. Dan and Julia just made my Christmas card list.

'No problem. Thought it might warm you up. They gave me that when I left Deloittes. Engraved and everything. No use for it myself but Julia likes a little perk every now and then, don't you darling?'

'Though never at this time in the morning,' clarifies Julia, reaching back to take the flask from me. 'I see you've emptied it.'

'Don't have the rest of the bottle handy do you?'

'Sorry?'

'Just joking. I'm feeling much better, actually. In fact I've just recalled my therapist's number. I'm supposed to call her if something like this ever happens. Do you have a phone I could borrow? I have mine with me but it's...well...'

I poke my soaked Nokia through a gap in the rug.

Esmie visibly recoils at the sight of it. 'You really *are* a time traveller,' she says. 'Did you drop that over the side of the Ark?'

'Perhaps I could borrow yours?'

'Er...like *no*.' Esmie curls a protective claw around her iPhone. Her eyes narrow suspiciously. 'You can't remember your own name but you can remember your therapist's number?'

'12345.'

'Congratulations on being able to count.'

'That's her number. 12345. She's a memory specialist after all.'

'What*ever*.'

'Esmie don't be so rude. Here." Dan reaches into his gilet and pulls out his phone. Unlocking it with his thumb he hands it over his shoulder to me, keeping his eyes tight on the road ahead.

'Thanks. You're all being very kind.'

'Don't mention it,' says Dan. 'We were heading into town anyway. Picking Esmie something for her birthday, hey love?'

'Nothing magnetic, I hope.'

'Dad!'

Julia snorts from the front, though quickly converts it into the appearance of a sneeze. Dan grins at me in the mirror but already I'm down at the phone, tapping away with newly thawed fingers.

Voicemail inbox first. Time to get a grip on this whole situation at the Ambassadeur. The facts are out there, and I've a funny feeling I'm going to need them soon.

I have two new messages. First one was left for me at 21.37 last night.

'Dark? Dark is that...oh bugger this thing.'

Babs.

'Um...yes. It's me again old chap. I do wish you'd pick up. I um...made that phone call like I promised and it's all a bit of a mess. Turns out your...um...'client' and Bill O'Malley have history, and not just all that stuff with the tower. Rumour has it that when O'Malley's not laying foundations for Terrata he's laying other men's wives. Right old sausage smuggler, apparently, Gary Chadwick's sister being a recent addition to the notches on his luxury bedpost. Flushed her marriage right down the pan. Women, hey? And men. Women and men. Bastards, the lot of them. Anyway, hope that's of use to you. Will get those papers you gave me to Spickle ay-sap. Now for god's sake get yourself home. Think what Felicity would say. And for Christ's sake leave that stringy Russian barmaid alone. Don't like the look of her at all. Anyway, jolly-ho for now. Nice to catch up and what have you. Now how do I get this bloody thing to...'

Interesting. I've never heard of Bill O'Malley but I know all about the bogeymen at Terrata. Not a month goes by on the island without some new architectural monstrosity of chrome and glass roaring up from the soil with the Irish developer's logo warted into its flank. Residential rabbit-hutches and office blocks are a speciality, as are the numerous foreign-owned multi-million pound piles that stud the island's coast like blocky gobs of phlegm hacked into the undergrowth by some champagne-snorting spiv. Terrata – a Finance-fed cancer gnawing hungrily away at what little character the island retains, unchecked, unstoppable, uncaring.

But what's all this to me? And who's Gary Chadwick? I'm pretty sure there's a politician of that name in the States, one of those green left-wing whingers that firms like Terrata like to grind down as mix for their concrete. Is that who Babs means?

'Everything ok back there?' asks Dan. We're heading down the long residential decline of Queen's Road and into town, bearing in on the northern outskirts of St Helier.

'Fine thanks. She's taking her time to answer.'

'No shit,' mutters Esmie, rolling her eyes.

The next voice message starts up. This one is logged as having come through at 22.04. For a moment there's merely silence and air and the hiss of what sounds like static. Then a male voice begins.

Mr Dark. Marigold Dark, it begins. The accent is soft but unmistakably Irish, the speaker's heavy breath carrying down the line. *Loik oy said before. Stay away from me...or oi'll have yer daughter.*

There's a hiss. A sharp scraping sound, like wood over stone. The message ends.

'...seriously Dad, he stinks...'

'...if you want that tablet you'd better...'

Esmie and Julia's bickering has assumed a garbled, underwater quality. We're sinking, car and all, down into dark and gloopy depths. Dan's head turns slowly, lips parting to release a low, whale-like drone. Something slick and slimy takes a chunk out of my guts.

What was that movie with Liam Neeson where they kidnap his daughter? The one where he bangs on about having a certain *skill set* and how he's going to find them and kill them all and so on? Because that's me right now. I'm Liam Neeson right now, though minus the *skill set* and any clue whatsoever about who or what or why this bastard is threatening Louise, threatening my daughter.

No *skill set*, no. Friends in unusual places, though. I've several of those.

'Change of plan,' I croak, heart thumping, mouth dry. 'Take me to the police station.'

'Um...okay.' Dan's brow furrows in the rear view mirror. 'Hey, are you sure you're warm enough back there? You're shivering again.'

Oi'll have yer daughter.

Not shivering, Dan. Shaking.

There's a difference.

5 – Cell Fun

Caged again. A welcome upgrade from the urine-soaked boot of a Renault Clio, nevertheless; I've room to pace this time, as well as a view out through some badly painted bars at a badly decorated corridor in the middle of which two police officers are trying their best to be pleasant. Badly.

'This way please Madam, if you wouldn't mind. That's it. Just in here. Mind your head. No madam, not that one, this one. The empty one.'

The *madam* in question catches my eye. Late forties, limp skin and grief, one of those thin ragged types God lowers to earth on sticks to mop up all the misery he spilt whilst making the place.

'Al'righ der mate,' she slurs, half-raising a hand in salute. Scouser. 'Lovin' the underpants 'n tha'. Real fuckin' action man.'

Placing a fist on either hip I strike a pose, stiffening my chin and gazing off into the distance a la Kayes Catalogue 1985. She likes that, lapsing into a rattling laugh that sounds like her entire insides just tore loose.

'Ah fuckin' *lov'* him,' she manages, as the female officers finally thread her sagging frame through the doorway of her cell. 'He's alrigh', dah one.'

'If you say so love,' says the taller of the two officers, a stern and rather bulky brunette. 'Others may disagree.'

PC Jan de la Haye always makes me think of horses. It's not so much the elongated face or the dark plaited hair (though there is that) but more the sheer size and force of her, the impression I always get that Jan is at her happiest when pushing, pulling or squeezing some other living organism into its allocated stall. Having been on the receiving end of those powerful hands more than once in the two years I've known her I never fail to suffer an involuntary tightening of my scrotum when Jan's within reach. They'd be retracting now, as it happens, had this morning's dalliance with the freezing elements not already sent them fleeing halfway up my chest.

The cell door slams shut on my Northern admirer. Dismissing her fellow officer with a curt nod Jan strides down the corridor towards me. Though my door's unlocked she chooses to address me through the bars, glaring down her sizeable nose at me like a primary school teacher who's just caught the class bully pants down in the sandbox.

'Please. Do the front of your gown up. All that white flesh is giving me a migraine.'

'Is he here yet?'

'He's coming. Just saying goodbye to those new friends of yours. Dan and...'

'Julia.'

'Julia. They weren't too impressed, by the way.'

'I'm not surprised. That reception area of yours needs painting and as for the furniture...'

'Not with *us*, love. With that stupid story you fed them. The memory loss routine. I left their darling daughter bellowing that she knew you were, and I quote, a "freaking weirdo" all along.'

'This is no routine, Jan. It *is* all a blank.'

'Oh I'm sure it is.' Jan folds her arms, cocks her head. 'We all

49

know that there's a test card – that little girl and her dolly – where the last few years' memories should be in whatever's left of your brain...'

'Wine bottles, Jan. A little girl surrounded' (*I'll do your daughter*) 'by empty bottles. No dolly.'

'...but certain things, however – your name, your address, your reason for being up on the north coast in nothing but those horrible Y-fronts of yours – certain things I find it hard to believe you've forgotten. So be a good boy and try to answer his questions, okay? You'll only make him angry otherwise.'

I love it when Jan gets all matriarchal like this. I never had a mother, not a *real* one with backbone and orders and genuine grit.

'Can I have a hug please?'

'Will a kick in the knackers do instead?'

I'm about to respond with something devastatingly funny when the doors at the far end explode inwards, spraying the corridor a bright shade of DCI Iain Ledger. At the approach of her chief Jan takes a step back from the bars of my cell and folds her hands behind her back.

Here he comes, my mate Iain. Iain-ee. The Ledgemeister. Big L. The Iainster.

'For Christ's sake, Dark,' he bellows, striding towards us down the hall in a wave of rage and high vis jacket. 'What the *fuck* are ye playing at this time?'

'I love this guy,' I whisper to Jan. For some reason she blushes. Looking over at Ledger their faces momentarily lock, causing her superior's stride to momentarily falter. It's the briefest of exchanges but I catch it – Jan turning to study an anti-drink drive poster on the wall, Ledger recovering himself with a moustache-bristling snort – I catch it all; the confused and awkward tenderness, that momentary slip of their professional masks.

Well then. That's handy to know.

'So then? Ya big twat.'

Ledger stands before me, hands on hips, face aflame. Looks like Super Mario on a bad day, my Iain. Looks like Super Mario would upon waking up to find that big spiky turtle thing has acquired the deeds to his house, Luigi's moved in with the Princess and Sonic the Hedgehog's done a shit in the bath. Glaswegian too, which makes it all the funnier. Stocky, short, and beneath that ever present police hat, bald, Ledger's got the classic Little Man syndrome nailed. Which is funny, as Iain rolls in at a perfectly respectable five foot eight, which must just piss him off all the more.

'Who are you again?' I ask. 'I'm sorry. I just...my memory, it's ...'

'Who am...who am *I*? Hmm. Let's see.' Ledger swings the cell door wide and steps in to join me. I gaze lovingly into the fury of his eyes, resisting the urge to take a step backwards as the peak of his police cap jabs my forehead. Nice cologne today. Lucky Jan.

'I'm the fucker that's kept you out of prison for these past few years,' Ledger fumes, his voice dropping almost to a whisper. 'I'm the guy that puts up with your crap, bails you out, scrapes the shite from the fan. *Your* shite. *My* fan.'

'All part of our...*agreement*, surely?

'Oh aye,' he mutters, lowering his voice with a brief glance at

Jan, who deftly turns away – 'but there are fuckin' *limits*, right? My colleagues aren't stupid. My colleagues aren't blind. You're not the States of Jersey Police *mascot*, for fuck's sake. And now...this.'

He motions at my near-nakedness.

'Lying in the middle of a fucking road in yer cacks. In November. Harassing the public...'

'They stopped for me. Voluntarily.'

'...claiming fucking memory loss. *Falsely* claiming memory loss when you know damn well who you are, as do the rest of us poor bastards that have ta put up wi' you.'

'Who am I then?'

'Marigold Dark. Part time 'private investigator,'' he sneers, inverting commas with his index fingers. 'Full time basket case. Constant, incessant – nay, fuckin' *agonising* – pain in my arse.'

'Has uses. Will travel.'

'*Marigold*.' Jan chimes in from the corridor. 'Marigold. Such an unusual name.'

'My parents were Manichean hippies.'

'United or City?'

'Jan love.' Ledger raises his palms as though attempting to arrest a toppling wardrobe. 'Jan. *Please*. Feel free to play Humour The Crazy Bastard in yer own time but please...right now I simply want some answers from this arsehole. Go grab the sorry twat some clothes from the store room. Shoes too.'

Thunderclouds roll across Jan de la Haye's face. She glares back with an expression of bruised hostility, as if daring him to say that again. If I ever needed confirmation that these two have got something going on I just got it.

'*Please*, Officer de la Haye,' says Ledger softly, realising his mistake. 'Clothes for our man here.' He glances back over his shoulder as though scared of what he'll find. 'Sub him a fiver too. Make sure he gets home.'

Jan gathers herself, though the clouds remain. 'Right away. Sir.'

There is silence as Jan leaves us, broken only by the sound of her boots on the floor and the grinding of Ledger's teeth. He keeps his eyes closed, head bowed as though in prayer until the clang of metal signals Jan's departure into the adjacent corridor.

Lover boy's for it later. Ouch.

'So then,' scowls Ledger, looking up at me. 'To what do I owe the acute displeasure?'

'I wanted to ask you something.'

'Oh did you now?'

'Bill O'Malley. Gary Chadwick.'

'What about them?' Ledger's eyes narrow beneath the peak of his cap.

'What's the link? I'm on a case. These two are involved somehow and...'

'You're on a fucking *case*,' Ledger laughs bitterly at the ceiling. 'Oh Christ you're on a *case* now are ye?'

'Someone threatened my daughter, Iain...'

'Dark...'

'What's the deal with these two? Fill me in. Help me to...'

'I'll fill yer arsehole with my boot,' sighs Ledger, 'is what I'll do. Right up past the fuckin' laces.'

'Rather unprofessional of you.'

'What's unprofessional, Dark, what's un-pro-fuckin'-

fessional is me standin' here entertainin' a fuckin' *madman*, is what.'

'And there was me thinking we were friends.'

'Ever the fuckin' optimist, hey Dark. But listen.' Ledger steps back to lean against the bars of the cell, his arms folded. 'I've got a question for *you*. Yesterday lunchtime – one oh eight to be precise – we get a phone call from a member of the public reportin' some suits having a set-to on the terrace outside Alfred's restaurant. Turns out to be dear Mr Chadwick and a certain Irish property director. Lobster flying and all sorts. Proper fuckin' *spat*. All caught on CCTV as well.'

'You pulled them in?'

'Not yet. No-one's reported a crime as such, except our friend on the phone – got lobster juice on his pinstripes, poor wee bastard – and you know how it is over here when dealing with politicians and the like. Can't just wade in there. We'll most probably be having a 'quiet word' with the two of them later today. For now though we're just going through the video, working out what happened, getting our facts straight.'

'Facts are useful things.'

'Ay, Dark, that they are. Hence my detecting the merest glimmer of a silver lining to the massive fuck-off cloud presented by your reappearance in this building. 'Cos I'm hoping you can...*enlighten* me a little on what set the whole spat off.'

'You want me to play Holmes to your Watson? Dig out my trench coat and cigar? Throw some CSI shapes at the video tape?'

'Something like that will do, Dark,' scowls Ledger, waving a fag-yellowed finger in my face. 'Because it was you that threw the lobster, ya useless wee prick. You were bloody well *there*.'

6 – Lobster

Horrible thing, blackmail. Especially when it involves nice, rosy-cheeked ladies like Ledger's wife Veronica. Let's hope that Super Mario here isn't planning to turn up the heat on this latest lobster-hurling revelation. I'd hate to have to drag him into the pot with me.

I've met Ronnie Ledger a couple of times, the last and saddest occasion being her brother-in-law Philip's funeral. I can still recall those big leaky eyes peering down at me as I lay there in the aisle, my left arm bent beneath me, a bubble of vomit popping soundlessly upon my lips. To my lasting shame I'd been unable to resist a quick peak up her skirt (black tights, vast thighs) before Iain had hauled me to my feet and thrown me out into the rain, instigating a second and rather less dramatic tumble down the church steps and into the side of an idling hearse.

Philip Ledger and I had got on okay, and so making my way down to St Luke's church to pay my respects had seemed like a reasonable enough thing to do. Unfortunately for the Ledgers, the vicar and the attended congregation I'd heard that pesky God of theirs bellowing Let There Be Rum Wrapped in Brown Paper on the way into town and half a bottle later lo! down I'd gone at Ronnie's feet.

The wonky pews and slippery flagstones hadn't helped. Dreadfully uneven they were, all pocks and potholes. I'd penned a letter of complaint to the parish soon after but couldn't find a stamp. Couldn't find the letter either.

The *first* time I'd set eyes on Veronica Ledger was back around the turn of the decade, having popped in unannounced one day to bug her house.

The Ledgers had just arrived on the island, quietly beating a tactical retreat from their native Glasgow after a few unwise decisions had locked Iain's police tartans in spin-cycle with the bloodied grots of The Golden Bawbag (a local drug gang so-called after the gold-painted testicles of rival gang leader Jay 'T-Blade' McLeish were returned by post to his mother in a little ribboned box). I never did get to the bottom of Ledger's exact dealings with GB, nor how he ended up under their control, but whatever had happened, our Iain had been a silly boy, and now the Bawbag had him by the...well, *baws*.

Were Iain *actually* Super Mario he could simply have eaten a gigantic mushroom and stomped on their heads, though this being off the table fleeing the city had seemed the Ledgers' only legitimate option. Big brother Phil had been living the Jersey life for close to a decade already (working for a rival private fiduciary firm across the road from my own), so when a senior investigating post came up on the island Ledger had leapt for it. Transfer request approved, Uncle Iain and Auntie Vee had swapped sporrans for sandals and set up a new life on the largest of the Channel Islands faster than you could say 'compromised copper on the run from nut-chopping psychopaths'.

Alas, the best laid plans of swine and men. The Ledgers had been on the island barely a month before the first consignment of deep-fried heroin turned up on their doorstep, gift wrapped with love. This was the beginning of a fairly standard blackmail set-up – Iain was to assist the local force in turning a wee blind eye to Golden Bawbag's burgeoning Jersey operation and in return those dirty tartans of his would stay stuffed down the back of some grimy wardrobe in the Gorbels. Right next to that half-used tube of glitter-gold paint and that meat cleaver.

Having confessed his woes to brother Phil – the late night phone calls from untraceable Glasgow numbers, the damning photocopies delivered to the house, the nerve-sanding sense of being continually watched – Iain Ledger had begun the slow and painful process of logging off from his own life. The Golden Bawbag had him by the fuzz. Either he used his new position to help the Glaswegians foist their scag on Channel Islanders or he was finished; as a copper, as a husband, as a card-carrying, testicle-boasting male.

Cue me.

My entry to this sorry situation came via some work I'd done for a friend of Phil Ledger's. A standard adultery case; bugged phones, a few snaps of a hairy birth-marked arse through the wrong kitchen window and the case had been closed. For once I'd made a good job of it, and when Philip started putting out gentle feelers about local PIs it was my card that got quietly pressed into his palm.

When it came, Phil's emailed brief was simple – I was to gather as much information on the Jocks that were strapping his brother and then see what, if anything, could be done. All of this was to be conducted without Iain's knowledge, bugging of phones, email interception and stalking being generally frowned upon by those bugging, email-intercepting stalkers in blue.

The covert nature of my task meant that tapping Iain's house phone was a regrettable necessity. Getting into the

Ledger's house under the guise of an Estate Executor was easy enough; I'd had the company website and stationary made up a few weeks previous (GaynorRemaynes.com – 'we dish your wish'), all of which bore the logo of a silhouetted power-wrestler attempting to drag the corpse of a camel through the eye of a needle by its stretched and shattered neck (an ingenious design of which I'd been rather proud, even if it did become a bit blobby when reduced in size for letterheads and pens. T-shirts were fine though; I've still got one or two somewhere.)

'I didn't even know I had an aunt in Switzerland,' Veronica had muttered, kneading the folds of her chin whilst eying the numbers on an official looking document I'd run up hours before. I'd bluffed my way in as far as the lounge by now, successfully presenting as the sort of grey, faded man who runs errands for the dead and easily winning the confidence of my floral-decked hulk of a host.

'I'm not promising anything Mrs Ledger. Not before a cup of tea, anyway. And it *is* Victoria, yes?'

'Veronica.'

'Ah. So *that's* what the V stands for.'

'Is that a problem?'

'Possibly. Possibly not. Like I said, a tea would be lovely. And could I possibly use your phone? Just need to check with head office.'

'Of course.'

I'd had the device in place before she'd made it to the kettle. A small RF transmitter picked up off e-Bay; I had and still have a bag of them at home. In it went through the battery compartment as usual, an easy job provided enough booze has been sloshed back to steady the hands, which on that day it had.

One midnight raid on the Ledgers' rubbish bins later (Operation Phone Bill) and I had the name, number and Glasgow address of Iain's chief persecutor, Golden Bawbag head honcho and card-carrying nut job 'Gooey' Louis Lee. And the phone tap had worked a treat, allowing me to listen in on the late night instructions as they were delivered to an initially defiant though ultimately broken Ledger.

Basically thus: Gooey's eldest son Louis Jnr would be arriving in Jersey with the express intent of flooding our fair island with a wave of high grade tartan brown. The Jersey Police would, understandably, be trying to stop him. And in the middle of this was to be Ledger, tipping the scag-stained scales in favour of the Glaswegians. Failure to comply would result in a visit from old friends, scissors, gold paint etc etc.

Tipping scales is my forte, however, and Gooey Sr's side was coming right back at him. A few weeks spent fishing amidst the scum and bar-larvae with which I decorate my sorry life (or 'my friends' as they sometimes refer to themselves) turned up news that the first of Louie Jnr's scheduled late night beach-drops was about to go down. An unremarkable dish – speedboat from France, secluded cove, heroin handed over, sales, death, misery, weeping relatives, etc etc – favourably seasoned by a sprinkling of shredded pig.

Establishing the time and location of the Bawbag's drop had cost me a trip to the Toad. Hacker extraordinaire, wizard of the dark internet arts, digital hermit; John Spickle's been my go-to guy for years now. It's a mutually beneficial arrangement – we pariahs have got to stick together, after all.

Like me John used to have a wife and family, until the careless importation of some remarkably deviant videos cost him his senior position in the Data Commissioner's Office, since when he's spent his time holed up alone in a tiny cottage on the Noirmont headland, gaining excessive weight whilst squinting out over a screen bank worthy of NASA. Much of John's time is spent honing the complex FOREX algorithms with which he is rapidly making himself a very wealthy man; the rest is spent hacking to order, creating viruses and beating off to God knows what. Loves his weed, does fat John, when he can get it, which is whenever *I* can get it, which is whenever I need something from him.

Which I did, in this instance. Having dredged my fellow lowlife for the herbal goods I'd been forced to endure a moderately uncomfortable bus journey out to Noirmont with a funky smelling rucksack. The green had looked a little on the dry side to me but Spickle had been happy enough to take the lot in exchange for a thorough hacking of Louis' Jnr's phone, email and social media, from which he eventually managed to pull the time and location of the drop.

'Eathie,' Spickle had lisped, reaching round to scratch the bared canyon of his arse crevice as he peered into his screens. 'You want me to thtick a viwus in his in-bockth?'

'Why not,' I'd nodded, through the drifting haze of blazed ganja.

'I'll canthel his Netflickth subscwiption ath well. Pwick.'

Yup, saving Ledger's bacon had been an all round team effort. As well as enlisting the Toad I'd called in a favour from my old friend and occasional fixer Jean de Gruchy. Never one to suffer off-islanders/drug smugglers/the Scottish gladly my old friend the Farmer had been more than happy to lend me his three sizeable sons and within days the trap was set. Oscar, Jed and Devlin owed me a favour or two as it was, though I suspect the simple offer of a fight would have been enough to lure them off their father's farm and into their war paints.

Forty eight hours later found the de Gruchy boys playing midnight commando – black stripes across the nose, dark beanie hats, the works – on a remote stretch of the island's north coast.

They hadn't long to wait. Louie Jnr's little white van had pulled up right on time, and within minutes a powerboat could be heard buzzing in across the darkened waters. No sooner had the mucky bundles been transferred to the van and the speedboat bid farewell then Louie Brown Jnr and his two teenage assistants were ambushed, twisted into funny shapes and left to think things through in the bushes.

Their van we'd buried at an undisclosed spot on the Farmer's land, and Louie's heroin with it. Satisfied at a job well done Jean and I had clinked Calvados bottles as we'd watched young Jed's JCB carving out a trench in the moonlight. Framed by stars we'd stood, jaws jutting like wartime heroes as...

'Are you even fucking *watching*?' Ledger raps on the television screen with a knuckle. 'Earth to Dark. You there?'

We're in his office, looking over the CCTV from yesterday's incident on the terrace at Alfred's.

'I'm here.'

'Well fuckin' well pay attention.'

He gets like this, sometimes, does Iain. Forgets that

somewhere in a field in St Ouen his plastic-wrapped freedom is degrading on the back seat of an upturned white Suzuki. Forgets how I used it to blackmailed Gooey Louie Snr into leaving the Ledgers alone. Forgets how much he owes me.

I'll remind him, if I have to, like I've reminded him before. Like I say, it's not a nice thing, blackmail, and now, with this Jan thing...

'So then. Care to elaborate on this latest little *charade*?'

Clothed now in borrowed jog pants, black sweatshirt and flip flops I meet Ledger's eyes in the reflection of the monitor screen and wonder how much further I can push this. How much longer he'll tolerate my behaviour before taking his chances and planting a boot up my arse. The debt's paid, surely. I've still got some leverage but this handle's picked up a nasty wobble of late.

'Um.'

'Do you remember any of this at all?'

'Hmm.'

I turn my attention to the tape playing before me. Black and white footage. Wall mounted camera. Mute. We're looking down at Alfred's outside terrace. The white numerals 13.04 are visible in the corner. There's the tall, suited figure of Gary Chadwick sat stiffly at his table, hands gripping the arm-rest of his chair as though he's expecting to be vertically ejected at any moment. A wide-bellied walrus in a suit – late fifties, white moustache, vaguely recognisable – takes his seat opposite a woman at a table a metre or so away from the politician. Words have just been exchanged; the big guy's not happy with Chadwick about something.

'The fat bloke's O'Malley, I take it.'

'Correct.'

'Who's the woman?'

'No idea.'

O'Malley's dining companion; blonde ponytail hanging down the back of some expensive looking jacket, face obscured. She seems unperturbed by the ensuing inter-table barney, turning to reveal her profile and sizeable roman nose only when O'Malley gets back to his feet and takes a clear step towards Chadwick's table.

'This is the best bit,' mutters Ledger, tapping the screen with his biro.

For lo! Here I come, stumbling into frame, the collars of my trench coat raised, mouth working soundlessly. I'm staggering a little whilst swinging something that does very much indeed resemble a lobster around my head in the manner of a medieval flail.

'Crikey.'

'Not exactly *standard* adult behaviour, hey Dark?'

'Not *that*, Ledger. This bottle here.' I tap Chadwick's table on the monitor screen. 'We were drinking red wine with *fish*? You sure this tape hasn't been played with?'

'Fly Nemo, fly,' mutters Ledger, his eyes flashing as the shellfish projectile makes its short airborne journey across the screen and into O'Malley's face.

'Nemo was a fish, Iain.' One of Louise's favourite films, that. One of *mine*, come to think of it. We watched it five, six times. *Don't cry, Daddy, don't cry...*

'If ah say that lobster's called Nemo then it's called fuckin'

Nemo, right? *Super* fuckin' Nemo in fact. See the way it just knocked Bill O'Malley flyin'?'

The silent movie continues to play out before us like some piss poor reboot of *Laurel and Hardy*. The lobstered developer is down on the decking clutching his face. Chadwick – who in appearance actually isn't all that dissimilar to Stan Laurel – is on his feet. All heads turn as the waiters come running. I've already fled the scene, exiting screen right.

'Terrible waste of shellfish.'

'Assault, Dark, is what I'd call it. *Assault*.'

'O'Malley reported this?'

'Not yet he hasn't. Like I said before, *someone* did, a few minutes later. My bets are it's that chap there with the curly white hair. See? Took a right spattering when you ripped the lobster from his plate. Double-barrelled name. Finlay-something. Not important.'

'So now what?'

'That's up to Mr O'Malley.' Ledger pulls away, temples knitting in an attempt to impress severity. Adorable. I find myself fighting the impulse to reach up and tweak his cheek. 'Pinstripe splashin' isn't a capital offence in Jersey – yet – so on that score you're fine,' he continues, arms folded. 'Alfred's is private property so a charge of public disorder is tricky. Plus, seeing how O'Malley seems to have instigated things I'm sure you'll only argue that you were defending Mr Chadwick...'

'...I'd have thought that was obvious...'

'...so there's that. Ultimately the only way this is going anywhere is if O'Malley wants it to. We'll ask him when we see him.'

'What do you mean, 'when we see him'?'

'Well now,' says Ledger, his tone darkening. 'This is where it gets interesting. I'm sure you'll be thrilled to learn that O'Malley's been reported missing by his wife. You're looking at our last sighting of him *here*.' He taps the screen. 'It was Mrs O'Malley's birthday last night, poor love. Big party planned, surprise guests, balloons, streamers, all that *shite* – but old Bill never made it home. We've officers out looking for him now. Fancy that, hey Dark?'

'Right.' I follow Ledger's eyes as they laser-map my face. 'Fancy that.'

'Might be an idea to start working out what you did yesterday, hey? After...*this*.' He taps the monitor. *Clunk clunk.*

'I'll see what I can do.'

'Hour by hour. People. Places. Never know when that kind of info could come in handy. I'm sure Mr O'Malley's fine and all, but you know...'

'Gentlemen.'

We turn. Jan de la Haye stands in the doorway of the little office holding two mugs of tea. 'Thought you could do with something wet and warm inside you.' She catches Iain's eye and winks. 'Milk no sugar,' she adds, handing us a mug each. 'Like or lump.' Mine has a WW2 era logo on the side: KEEP CALM AND YOU'RE FUCKING NICKED, it reads.

Tea. Very funny.

'So I can go?'

'For now.' Ledger takes his mug from Jan. 'Thanks for that, officer. Ahem.' He winces as a wave of hot liquid splashes his fingers. 'Like I said, Dark. People. Places. Just in case. I'm fine,

Jan love...*seriously*.'

'But your hand. Here, let me...'

'I'm *fine*.'

How very awkward.

'I'll be off then,' I say, wincing to my feet. 'Good to see you both.'

Iain and Jan part uneasily to let me through. Neither speaks as I slide between them, mug in hand. Having reached the top of the stairs I turn to find them watching me in a tableaux of unease.

'You make a lovely couple by the way,' I say, raising a toast. 'Real cute.'

Ledger spasms like he's just been tasered in the nuts. Jan just stares down at the side of the filing cabinet. There they remain, frozen in place as though awaiting a painter to commit their guilt to canvas. I leave them like that, tramping down the stairs to reception, tipping my tea into the soil of a tired looking Yucca plant as I pass.

The clock on the corridor wall says it's fifty-seven minutes past ten. The pubs will be serving in **three**.

I pause for a moment in reception, considering my next move. I suppose I'd better get hold of Gary Chadwick, find out what exactly I'm supposed to be doing for him and what occasioned yesterday's lunch date. Get the low down on his beef with O'Malley. The pubs will be serving in

Two.

Answers. I need answers. Because this is quite a fix I'm in. *Something* drew me to the Hotel Ambassadeur last night, something important enough to warrant my being thrown from a cliff. On top of this I've managed to implicate myself in the assault and subsequent disappearance of a senior businessman. And worst of all, some anonymous scumbag is threatening the safety of my daughter, or worse.

Yes, I need answers, and fast. Marigold Dark, PI needs to get his act together. It's time to go to work. The pubs will be serving in

One.

7 – Cauliflower Omelette

Only I don't go straight to the pub. I don't turn left out of the police station car park, don't power-walk down to the western edge of town, definitely don't break into a jog as the town church strikes eleven and as such fail completely to clatter wheezing into the Shipwright for my first pint of the day.

There's just too much to be done, and this latest revelation about Bill O'Malley's disappearance has me rattled. I need to get my bearings. Only a sick shell of a man would bury himself in a pub with all this going on about him, a weak low-life with nothing going for his sorry existence save a functioning oesophagus and the ability to ferry liquid to his lips.

And I'm not that man. I have a mystery to unravel. I'm a private investigator on a case. And they threatened my daughter, damn it; they went and made it personal by threatening Louise.

Still, I *have* had quite a morning. With Ledger's five pound note I buy a bottle of South African red from the Portuguese mini-market on the corner of Charing Cross, unscrewing it in the aisle and dropping the cap to the floor. The Madeiran lady behind the counter tugs nervously at her braids as the change spills like metal rain from my shaking palm, clattering away from me across the counter. I thank her anyway and totter away mumbling.

At the edge of the park I sit on a bench in the rain and cry for a while, face hidden within the hood of my borrowed sweatshirt. It tumbles back after one particularly committed swig, allowing the sky's tears to join hands with my own for a slow waltz down my cheeks. I hear a motorbike approaching, realise that the low rumble of its engine is actually coming from my throat and then erupt hysterically, firing warm snot down the length of the bottle, my face a hot mess of crumpled sobbery.

Here we are again.

Across the road the brown façade of the General Hospital scowls down at me through the trees. They're healing the sick in there. Anti-biotic drips. Kidney dialysis. Leg casts. Stuff that can be treated. Things that can be *fixed*. Things not like me.

I thump myself in the face. I'm aiming for my brain to be exact, though as usual all that skin and gristle and bone gets in the way. Momentarily dazed I study the little glass animal in my hand, lighter now that it has spit its beautiful poison down my throat. Only now do I truly notice its full physical presence, the weight of green glass in my hand, the sour taste of the wine in my mouth.

Who can fix *this*?

The pavement can, and does, the empty bottle shattering with a sound like a bus-load of fairies being driven into a wall. Instantly the rain is on the wreckage, rubbing its muzzle across the shards. What little red wine was left sniggers quietly into the gutter. I give it a wave, and in the motion of my arm and hand there is something of love, something by way of a reconnection with the universe. I imagine the little wine molecules peering round their new sewer home and squealing with delight at all that space, rushing off eagerly to make new friends.

Go, little wine molecules, be gone. The world is yours. I

stumble to my feet and roar at the sky, drawing glances from assorted passers-by. Fuck you all.

That's better. The wine molecules in my belly have made themselves comfortable in my gut; rugs, cushions, the works. Smiling grimly (for how else can one smile?) I hoist my hood and trudge off into the greyed streets of St Helier's pedestrian precinct. The shops are open, a moribund mope of slow-moving shoppers pecking weakly at their doors. Jewellery flashes behind reinforced glass. Bowed white faces on wet kagools. (Love that word. *Kagool. Kagoooooooool.*) The stone *crapaud* hunches on its marble plinth as though blasted by the wand of some wicked witch whilst trying to leap away from this shit-hole of a high street. Where's your kissing princess, little toad? Where's *your* fairytale ending? Twat.

I slip into Mothercare, spend a few minutes scanning the girls' clothing section and trying not to fall over. Louise will be too old for this stuff now, yes? What is she, five? Six? I catch her looking up at me through that brutal fringe inflicted on by her mother, the one that made her look like that pop star she used to sing along to; Jesse someone. *All about the money*, like this whole wretched world. Only that isn't Louise, that's someone else's little girl, running back to the till and the safety of her mother's legs as a troupe of little regurgitated wine molecules scurry down my chin.

I'm torn between two t-shirts – Peppa Pig or Minnie Mouse? I run my fingers over the bright colours and wonder why I never got round to buying Louise a nice t-shirt like this, why nice things were generally her mother's department. I gave her a Little Mermaid figure once (found beneath the dartboard at the Shipwright, a little chewed but still play-with-able), which only made her mother mad because *you never know who had it before* – or up whose arse it had been, presumably. Pictures; I remember drawing a few pictures, but buying toys, books, t-shirts like this...not my thing. Nice things never were.

Not on my radar. Not on my watch.

Just never seemed to happen.

She loved me though! She loves me. And I love her.

Good old wine. I'm smiling through tears at the counter assistant, who has a face a bit like Miss Piggie off *The Muppets*. All round and chubbery.

'Can I help you Sir?'

'*Can I help you Sir?*' I mimic her high voice right back at her, screwing my face up into my best Miss Piggie impression and staggering back into a row of tiny coats. She goes white. They don't have security guards in Mothercare. They should. She looks for one anyway.

But I'm off, back out in to the rain. I'm feeling much better now, thanks for asking. There's a song in my head, *Looking For Linda* by some random eighties' pop group. Who was it? I can't remember. I wonder if the Mothercare lady's name was Linda and I've psychically picked up on that through her fear. I often wonder whether I'm more psychically attuned then most. I sometimes wonder whether I have the 'gift' and that my addiction to alcohol is simply my mind's way of protecting me from going mad at the full and unbearable knowledge of the world that this gift will bring.

I pause by the post box outside WH Smith and vomit into the gutter.

Luckily for me I find my flat in its usual place on St Marks Road, a ten minute hobble up and away from the precinct. Like most others this end of town the building is a blocky Georgian affair, its magnolia shoulders hunched halfway down a drab and rather serious row. Mine's the middle floor, spread thick like misery-flavoured jam between two slices of younger and more upwardly mobile bread.

The couple above me do something requiring them to put on suits each morning; Finance drones, I think. The girl below is a recently qualified dentist. We've got this running joke going, me and the dentist girl; every time I meet her coming up or down the stairs I stretch my mouth open as far as it will go and say 'aaaaahhh,' whilst giving her a guided tour of my molars as she passes.

At least I think we've agreed it's a joke. I've never thought to check with her and she does move rather fast. Nice girl. Moving out soon, I gather. I heard her sobbing the news to her mother on the phone last week, having woken on the carpet outside her flat with the left half of my face gummed to the door. My natural inclination as a father had been to barge in and comfort her, though after the trouble I got into last time I'd decided to simply crawl back up the stairs to my flat.

Now I pause outside her door, craning an ear to make sure she's alright. She has music on. What *is* that? Carpenters? Adele? Sad music. Music to wipe your eyes to. I send a quick 'aaahhhh' through the door to make sure she knows I'm

73

thinking about her and continue on my way.

The lock to my flat where I left it, about halfway up the door, just under the handle. The relevant keys, however, are in my clothes back at Yola's flat.

Oh well. Throwing my weight against the door I shoulder through into the short hallway, returning only to nurse the oft-snapped wood back into its casing with my palm.

Staggering through the debris of the lounge to the kitchen I fetch myself a can of Stella from the fridge, lobbing the scrunched can on to the pile of unwashed clothing in my sink when I'm done. As my eyes roll back into focus I spy a crumpled piece of A4 paper pinned to the fridge door by a small magnetic frog. *Dear Mr Dark*, it reads, in printed font:

I have urgent need of your services and was hoping that we could meet on the terrace at Alfred's at 1pm tomorrow afternoon. Naturally I will pay for your time and efforts. I will be wearing an orange tie and shall make sure to have a copy of the Guardian laid square against the corner of the table. If you have not made yourself known to me (discreetly, please) by 13.15 then I shall leave and make one final attempt at effecting a rendezvous.

Yours sincerely,

GC

Gary Chadwick, I presume. Looks like I just identified my current client. How and when did this letter arrive? I really should invest in a diary.

My stomach bubbles. I should eat something. The options are limited; my fridge is little more than a cold, vertical dustbin, a sad place where good food comes to die. After a quick rummage through the rot and dewed cellophane – and after a brief though conclusive consideration of a semi-liquefied peach – I manage to retrieve a vaguely edible cauliflower and some eggs.

Cauliflower omelette it is then. I break two eggs into a glass, sprinkle in a little Tabasco sauce and hurl the slimy concoction back in one. Now for the cauliflower. Picturing the vegetable as the physical manifestation of my brain I take two large chomps, one to the area where I imagine the memories to be stored, the other at the front, my visual cortex. Alas, both memory and vision persist.

Mouth flushed out with one more Stella I slide the SIM card and battery from my recently deceased Nokia and grab a new casing from the drawer. A quick fiddle later and the phone blazes to life like a tiny plastic Phoenix. I dial up my voicemail, listen to that message again without teenage gingerference.

Loik oy said. Oi'll have yer daughter.

That voice is vaguely familiar. An older man, definitely. There's a Southern Irish curl to the words – could this be Bill O'Malley? – but the delivery is oddly strained, with the speaker clearly out of breath. I listen beyond it, trying to pick out the hissing noise in the background. There's an odd echo going on as well, as though the voice is bouncing off tiles.

Oi'll have yer daughter.

I sink to the couch, allowing the phone to tumble to the floor. I'll need to get a warning to Louise's mother. But how?

I've no idea what her new number is and there's that injunction to contend with. Two hundred metres or something. I suppose I could always shout.

I try to recall the last time I saw my daughter. Ah yes. A few months back. *Almost* got to see her that time. Made it as far as the science block before being taken down by the Deputy Head. An ex-professional rugby player, apparently; had his fill of fondling his beefy friends before moving into teaching instead. I suppose it's handy to have strongmen like that in a school, especially when you've got drunken parents climbing over fences and wailing down the corridors screaming *LouiseLouiseLouise*. There aren't many teachers these days with the skill set required to escort a grown man off the premises by his ears.

I give a large cauliflower-scented sigh. If I'm not allowed to see Louise then the least I can do is protect her from out here, in the field. I need to find out who's responsible for this message, and fast. And that means working out what drew me to the Hotel Ambassadeur last night.

I grab another Stella from the fridge. Something to chew on as I think this through. Brain oil. I've only just got comfortable on the couch when the hot press of my bladder derails my train of thought. I'm drowsy now, eyes closed, and it's only smelly water so I let I go, enjoying the bath-like warmth as it seeps through Ledger's jogging bottoms.

The couch will survive. I've some Shake 'n Vac in the kitchen.

I pass out.

Somewhere far away my phone is ringing.

8 – Salma

The Nokia giggles hysterically to itself as I snatch it from the floor and squint up at the screen. I don't recognise the number.

'Hello?' I croak, shuffling up into a crouch. Head's banging like a caged bull in a thunderstorm; mouth tastes like I've been chewing on a corpse. My soaked, clinging trousers have grown cold – suggesting I've been out some time – yet somewhat bizarrely I've acquired a hard-on.

'Mr Dark?'

'Who's this?'

'Gary.'

'Gary?'

'Chadwick.'

'Right.' I force myself up, shuffling my wet trousers free via a weird kind of slow motion jog whilst swigging the remnants of my last Stella. My underpants follow.

Erection, room. Room, erection.

'I'm not sure if you've...ah...heard the news.' Chadwick's voice – at once familiar and unknown – is crisp with anxiety.

'The news.'

'About Bill O'Malley. After yesterday's antics at Alfred's I thought that perhaps I'd better let you know that he was, you know...'

'Missing?'

This erection has me baffled. I give the end a few tugs, wondering whether I've the energy to masturbate. As if suddenly aware of its owner's intention it begins to sag and wilt.

Great. Face-palmed up by my own penis.

'It's worse than that, I'm afraid. I have it on good authority that they've found him. Or rather his...'

There's a pause at the end of the line. Chadwick's voice drops to a near whisper as he leans into the phone.

'...rather his *body*. Bill O'Malley's dead, Dark.'

'Dead,' I repeat, watching my erection fading into the palm of my hand like a salted albino slug. 'And the body turned up where?'

'Out on the North coast, not far from Corbet's Folly. Not quite sure of the details but it looks like someone dropped him over the edge. Of course it could be suicide but my source tells me that he'd taken a bit of a bashing before, um, before...you know.'

Corbet's Folly. An image returns to me of the beaten up Martello tower I'd spied along the cliff top this morning. That's the one, yes? Been in the news recently about some planned redevelopment that's got the Lefties up in arms.

I cast my mind back to this morning, my fake execution...had O'Malley's pasty corpse been churning in the foam beneath me all the while?

'Time of death?'

'No idea. The body's only been discovered this past hour.'

'Word travels fast.'

'It does when you've got friends in the Force. I probably shouldn't have said that, by the way.'

'No. You probably shouldn't.'

'Well, whatever. It is what it is. Thought the least I could do was...um...'

'Warn me.' It doesn't take a genius to spot the connection between my near-death experience and O'Malley's upgrade to *actual*. I've a feeling Chadwick's right; we're snagged on something nasty here. 'You say he took a bashing before he died. His injuries...were they...*lobster*-shaped?'

'What? Oh *that*. No, this has nothing to do with yesterday's fiasco. No, from what I gather O'Malley took a *proper* beating before he died. That incident at Alfred's though...doesn't *look* too good for us, does it? Not now.'

'Now what?'

'Now the man that you publically assaulted has turned up dead!' Chadwick drops to a whisper again. '*Murdered* even.'

'Mr Chadwick...is there someone there with you?'

'No. I'm here in the kitchen, my wife's upstairs in the bath and the kids are...why?'

'You keep lowering your voice.'

'Well you never bloody well know, Dark,' hisses the politician. 'It's just all a bit...*unsettling*. O'Malley and me have been publically at each others' throats for months now over this whole Corbet's Tower thing, and then yesterday at Alfred's, and then...*this*.'

Chadwick's right. I don't like the way this is heading either. Not to keen on this Stella, either.

'Mr Chadwick. Where did you go after Alfred's yesterday?'

'Back to the States, of course. We had an afternoon sitting to get through. Hundreds of marvellously interesting things to debate. An island to run.'

'And after that?'

'Home to my wife. Dropped my son at Sea Scouts around

half six, back to fetch him around eight.'

'Then?'

'Book then bed, Dark, as bloody usual. Latest biography of Gerald Durrell, if you're interested.'

'I'm not.'

'So what are you driving at?'

'Your wife. Heavy sleeper?'

'I don't really...I mean...what are you...?'

'And by that I don't mean is she a big girl, I'm asking whether she can vouch for you being beside her the whole night?'

'I don't bloody know! Short of waking her up every ten minutes and waving at her I don't see how...'

'Where do you live?'

'St Mary's. But what...'

'Five minute drive to north coast then. Roads empty at night. Straight there, straight back.'

'Are you seriously trying to suggest that I...that anyone could think for a bloody moment that I could have...?'

'A jury might. There's motive, yes?'

'Are you fucking *serious*, Dark?'

'Just saying that we need to talk.'

Chadwick exhales loudly, his desperation fluttering down the line. I imagine him in his kitchen, forehead to the wall, suddenly aware of its paper thinness, the slow spread of invisible cracks. I'm getting flashes; an unused milk urn stuffed with back issues of the *National Geographic*, an aging hi-fi with sellotaped yet still functioning tape deck, scattered moccasins by the door. See? Psychic.

'Fine,' he says, after an audible sigh. 'Somewhere...discreet. I'll come to you. To town, I mean.'

'The Duke of York. Half an hour.'

'The Duke of York? You think a...you think a *pub* is the best place to meet? I know it's at the arse end of town, but still...'

'We won't be seen. The York's basically a cave with carpet. None of the locals are going to recognise your face in there. They barely recognise their own. Just don't wear a suit.'

'Right. See you there.'

'Bye.'

Cheered by the prospect of a living, breathing pint I bring a fresh can of Stella into the shower with me and use its contents to shampoo my scrotum. I have no idea why I do this. Having patted myself dry with the dry(ish) corner of a mushroomy towel I triumphantly haul on some grey flannel trousers and a blue pullover. Smart enough.

Time to brave the bathroom mirror. It's not a pretty place to be. The bridge of my nose is swollen and purple from its encounter with Andre's forehead, my lower face is a mesh of small bramble cuts and that antifreeze has done something weird and crusty to my lips. My eyes remain swollen and baggy from this morning's weeping and I haven't shaved in days. Think I've chipped a tooth as well.

Other than that, it's all good.

Duke of York here we come.

But first.

It takes me a few minutes to locate the MacBook on the bedroom floor beneath a pile of week-old newspapers. Setting it on my lap I prize it open like some white plastic clam. My screensaver blinks on and there's Louise, grinning with wrinkled nose through a face of chocolate ice cream. Taken a few years back, this one, up at that place with the wheat maze.

I feel my eyes misting over. Look at her, the little tyke. Just *look* at her.

To work. I run a quick Google search of Gary Chadwick. Local born. Geography teacher in a previous life. Operated a part time bonsai import franchise for a while, real small branch. Ran for Deputy in one of the country parishes two years on the row, voted in second time round after his chief rival got done for DIC two days before the election. Environmentalist with a capital E. Wave turbine fanatic. Card carrying member of the National Trust. Frequently found sounding off in the States Chamber or blogging online about the overdevelopment of this *zone of bling, this septic isle* (his words). Frequently ignored, often pilloried by the pinstripe brigade. Married, three children, wife of twenty-two years. Very much the family man. Founder of the Facebook group staunchly opposed to the redevelopment of the Martello Tower known as Corbet's Folly. Enjoyed *Doctor Who* last Saturday night. Working through the *Harry Potters* with his seven year old son in an attempt to wean him off his Spiderman fixation. Had salmon for dinner two nights ago, picture taken, *isn't wife a star*. Hated Candy Crush at first but *oh my it's addictive.* Thinks the Minister for Economic Development looks a bit like Uncle Albert from *Only Fools and Horses,* comparative pictures posted. Recently 'liked' one of those internet *Downfall* parodies in which Hitler is informed that Terrata's latest housing scheme has been approved (not a bad one, either – Bill O'Malley is even name-checked by a subtitled Goebbels) and then there's another one about X-Factor, which is less funny, though a link in the comment section leads to some interesting and recently released home footage of one of this year's hopefuls giving a blowjob to his boyfriend whilst in the side bar there's a link to the Ten Photographs Taylor Swift Doesn't Want You To See and after that The Cast of *Teenage Mutant Ninja Turtles* Then And Now before I notice that they've omitted Louise's mother from a slideshow of the Seven Female Horror Monsters That You Should Definitely Avoid though I'm pleased to see my current girlfriend Salma Hayek is in there as the queen vampire from *From Dusk Till Dawn* because i always had a crush on Salma always had a thing for the latino types in general in my youth before my libido got snapped so long as they made sure to shave the right places because i never was a big fan of body hair on women, and those dark haired latino types have to watch it and i wonder if there are any pictures of a younger salma hayek with her boobs out but there's got to be because this is the internet after all

9 – Dealing in the Dark

There aren't any. Naked photos of Salma Hayek, that is. At least none that I can find in the fifteen minutes before I snap from my slick-chinned trance to find myself running embarrassingly late for my meeting with Gary Chadwick. Shedding the laptop I stumble from the flat and half leap / half fall down the stairs, pausing only to bear my molars to the frightened looking girl in the hallway as she cringes into the wall.

'Aaaaaaaah!'

Chadwick's been waiting twenty minutes by the time I join him in the York. A welcome antidote to the smug, mirrored lounges and faux-speakeasies of St Helier's financial district the York's like something that haemorrhaged up from Middle Earth. Patterned red carpet. Dark walnut everything. Framed sketches of nineteenth century riflemen doing nineteenth century things. A smattering of grey men fading softly into their early afternoon beer.

And there at the bar, sticking out like a gay Orc amongst Mormon Dwarves is our man Chadwick, making a pretty hideous job of leafing nonchalantly through *The Sun*. In the name of social camouflage he's made a desperate lunge at street wear; green and grey camo trousers, blue hooded top and a Chicago Bulls baseball cap, though the overall effect is more dud than blud. He looks like someone on day release. And he's drinking orange juice with a straw. Christ.

'Mr Dark,' says Chadwick, removing his cap and extending a hand. His smile wobbles nervously as I approach. He has a long, thin head slightly kinked above the ear – as though it's suffered one solitary though conclusive slam in a car door – whilst his solid, greying comb-over does little to mask an unusually high forehead. An awkward looking chap.

'Glad you could make it.' Chadwick blinks heavily. His handshake is clammy and limp. 'You're looking...*calmer* than when we last met.' He pulls a red handkerchief from his pocket and dabs at his nose. 'Excuse me. Had this bloody cold for days.'

'Carling please,' I inform the barman, a young Portuguese chap with sideburns you could hang mugs from. This time of day calls for Guinness but I'm unwilling to wince through the watery muck variant they pour here. I order the lager safe in the knowledge that I know I won't be disappointed; Carling tastes equally foul wherever you drink it. And sure enough.

'Mr Chadwick.' I begin, with a practiced gravity reserved for paying clients.

'As I said yesterday, it's Gary, please. Shall we?'

We move over to a small table by the window. An old Whitney Houston ballad bleeds from the pub speakers. There's a clink of balls from the pool table. Someone coughs and shouts *Derek, Derek*.

'We find ourselves in an uncomfortable situation, yes?' Chadwick splays his hands on the table and sighs.

'My situation has been uncomfortable for years, Mr Chadwick.' I raise my lager to the light, momentarily losing the politician's face in its weakly bubbling flank. 'Cheers.'

'Did you make any progress at the hotel?'

'The Ambassadeur?'

'Yes.'

'And?'

'And.' I roll the conjunction around my outstretched lower jaw like a marble. '*Aaaand.*'

'And *what*, Mr Dark?' Chadwick's irritation rises. 'What happened? Did you get to the bottom of this bloody video thing or not?'

'Video thing,' I repeat slowly, watching the bubbles rising in my pint glass. 'Vid. E.O. Thing.'

'For god's sake man!' hisses Chadwick, drawing glances from several of the Canon's grizzled patrons. He leans in closer, voice lowered. 'Video thing. With that bloody...with the *dog*.'

'The dog.' I've no idea what he's talking about, though didn't my Not-So-Long-Haired Lover from this morning mention something about a dog? *You want to know if I've seen any dogs recently. If I know anyone in hotel with bloody...*

'Labrador?'

'For Christ's sake, man!' Chadwick attempts to mute me with a swipe of his palm. 'Keep your bloody voice down.' He glances nervously round the pub, where nobody gives a toss. Over by the window an old woman rolls a cigarette. The barman's picking quietly at his phone.

'No dogs at the Ambassadeur, Gary. That's a negative.' Indulging his paranoia I lower my voice to a whisper. 'This...*video*, though. I think I need to see it again.'

Chadwick's thick lips tremble soundlessly. His eyes meet mine, the question clear; *are you serious?* For a moment I've the horrible feeling that he's going to bolt. He rises from his stool –

causing me to rise with him – though it's only to fumble around in his pocket for his Samsung smart phone. We sit down again.

'Damn it, Dark.' Chadwick weighs the device in his hand like some modern day Hamlet. *To see or not to see.* He sighs. He shakes his head. I'm intrigued.

'You want me to help you, yes?'

'But you've already *seen* the bloody thing,' he mutters.

'I need to see it again, I'm afraid.'

The politician grinds his teeth, causing a vein in his temple to bulge and flare. 'Here,' he says suddenly, handing over the phone. 'God knows why you'd want to put yourself through this again but if you think it will help...'

The MP4 recording is ready to play. Thirty-six seconds long, according to the scroll bar, of which the first five have already ticked by. I settle back into my seat, eyes on the Samsung's tiny screen.

So far, nothing. Just blackness, until the lens is pulled free from wherever to reveal a blue carpet with an orange floral design. There's the toe of a boot as our film-maker brings us closer to the foot of a bed. Jerkily up now, the lens rising to reveal that we are in a hotel room – small mounted television, rudimentary dressing table, wall mirror, shabby curtains, drawn.

Fifteen seconds gone. Night time? Hard to tell; the only light in the room comes from two mounted lamps above the headboard of the bed, on which two supine figures can be discerned. One of these is a large golden Labrador, half asleep or most probably sedated; it pants lightly on its side, black eyes half shut, pink tongue lolling from its jaw.

The other figure is a long, naked male whom at first glance

appears to be spooning the dog in a semi-affectionate manner, the fingers of his left hand buried deep in its thick, glossy fur.

Twenty four seconds gone. Now the camera zooms shakily in on the dog's rear, shifting its angle to reveal a surprising depth of connection betwixt man and beast.

Beside me Chadwick lets out a low, pitiful moan.

Thirty seconds gone. The lens retracts, moving up to linger on the sleeping politician's face – because yes, it's Gary Chadwick – upon which there rests a peaceful, dream-cushioned expression, as though its owner is innocently running in slow-mo down some vaseline-lensed beach, or slumbering blithe in some Caribbean hammock, far from the dog-arsed hotel room horrors awaiting his inevitable return.

Thirty-six seconds gone.

End of clip.

I experience a judder of *de ja vu*. I've seen this video before. Yesterday, at Alfred's. The memory returns in snatches; Chadwick insisting I take the smart phone into a toilet cubicle for a private screening...returning to the terrace to find Bill O'Malley hurling abuse at my client...the lobster snatched from a nearby table...

'Good looking dog, that.'

'*Isn't* it, Dark?' Chadwick's lips are thin, his fingers white where they clutch the table's edge. 'You know, that was the first thing that struck me when they emailed me the video. *What a bloody nice dog that is*, I thought. I even called Alice and the kids into my study to show them. *Have a look at this dog*, I said. *Isn't it lovely? That coat. Those eyes. I wouldn't be surprised if this dog has won the odd competition or two.* And that's when Kevin –

he's my youngest, Dark, only twelve, they get real curious at that age – that's when Kevin – scamp that he is – asked me to explain why it was that I had my ruddy *cock* up its fucking *arse*.'

I wipe the spittle from my cheeks. Chadwick sinks back into his seat and covers his face with his hands. The barman looks up from his phone. Heads creak slowly back into orbit around the rims of pint glasses.

'You think this is O'Malley's doing?' I ask, dealing in the dark.

'Of course it is. Was.' Chadwick looks up with wet eyes. 'He denied it yesterday at Alfred's – got angry when I threatened him with legal action – but it *has* to be Terrata. Who else?'

'Motive?'

'My opposition to their plans for Corbet's Tower, for starters. Plus we've never got on. Personal stuff.'

'Your sister.'

Chadwick sits up, startled. 'How the bloody hell do you know about that?'

'It's what you're paying me for, right? To dig. I dug.'

'Well yes, but...look...just leave my sister out of this. That has nothing to do with it.'

'Except motive, of course. You were drugged, I'm guessing?'

'When?'

'Lassie. The dog. They drugged you.'

'Of *course* they bloody...' Heads are turning again. Chadwick catches himself. Takes a deep breath. Continues. 'We went over this yesterday,' he scowls. 'Or were you too drunk to remember?'

'I remember everything, Mr Chadwick,' I nod, picking at

something white and crusty on my sleeve. 'It's just my *modus operandi*. Question everything. Then question it again. Wait for it to get comfortable and then pop back to question it again. One more thing and all that. You ever watch *Columbo*?'

'Yes, Mr Dark. But I was never a fan.'

'Shame. Peter Falk is a hero of mine.'

They'd had the complete *Columbo* on DVD in the television room at Wallace Lodge. Every afternoon Babs and I would watch an episode, slamming imaginary shots of whiskey (in our case cold tea) every time Columbo popped back for 'one more thing.' I became fixated, hauling myself hand over hand through each long dry day with Falk's beige trench coat as my rope. I think I even loved him for while. And then my time at Wallace Lodge ended and I ran straight to the nearest pub and that was that. I never watched *Columbo* again.

'One more time then, for the sake of clarity. Explain if you would how you came to have your John Thomas rammed up a Labrador's jacksy.'

Chadwick shudders. Takes a deep breath. Locks his fingers and leans in over the table so that our faces are but inches apart.

'Last Friday evening. I was at a fundraising event at the Hotel Ambassadeur. Little Cubs, a Down Syndrome charity I've been involved with for a few years. Our middle child Anna is...well, you know. Anyway. I'd been asked to give a brief speech during coffee, which I did, and then the DJ came on and myself and a few of the others hit the residents' bar. Alice was at home with the kids and so I was off the leash, so to speak.'

'An unfortunate metaphor, but go on.'

'So – as you should already know, Mr Dark – around

elevenish this swish young chap approaches me, leads me by the elbow into a corner. Introduces himself as Matt somebody, starts going on about Terrata's plans for Corbet's Folly, all that. Says he's outraged by the way our island heritage is being sold up the river. Says he knows that I'm one of the most vocal objectors in the States. Tells me that he has some information about Terrata that may be of interest to me. 'Potential leverage' he calls it, something to do with dodgy books or some such. Says if I've a few minutes spare he's got some documents in his room I might like to see.

'Well, bloody idiot that I am I agree. He buys us both an expensive whiskey and off we toddle to room something or other, pausing on the way to clink glasses and toast the success of Little Cubs or something and then *wallop* – down goes the whiskey. I remember thinking at the time that it tasted a bit off but...well. He starts fiddling with his room key, I suddenly start feeling a little bit worse for wear and next thing I know I'm waking up naked in a hotel bed with a horrible smell in the air and dog...' here Chadwick's voice drops to a whisper, '*dog shit* on my...on my...'

'I understand. And the rest? No recollections at all?'

'Blank. All a bloody blank. Of course Alice was livid when I got in. She'd reported me missing and everything. I pleaded inebriation but I don't think she bought it. Spent the next few days desperately trying to work out what had gone on until a few days later this...*delightful* little home movie pops up in my inbox. Unknown sender, just some random-lettered hotmail account with one message. NO MORE CORBET'S TOWER, MR CHADWICK. GIVE IT UP. That's all it said.'

'And have you?'

Chadwick closes his eyes, stewing in a marinade of his own misery.

'I think so, Dark,' he says, pinching his brow. 'If this gets out I'm ruined. My family, my career, my life in general. All over. What options do I have?'

'Is that a rhetorical question?'

Chadwick sighs. Straightening his back he lays his palms flat on the table before him. 'Mr Dark. I have it on good authority that you're a man who gets things done. Someone not afraid to...*blur the lines*, shall we say. Like I said yesterday, I was prepared to pay you good money to effect some sort of...counterbalance. Once we'd ascertained for certain where this...' He taps his Samsung, '...*muck* came from.'

'*Prepared*? I can't help but notice your use of the past tense.'

'O'Malley's death changes things. Now I'm not sure what to do. And as for you, Mr Dark...I'd heard good things, but right now I'm...'

'Right now you're what?'

'I don't know.' Chadwick runs a trembling hand across the glistening bowl of his forehead. 'What a bloody mess,' he mutters to himself, staring morosely at the table.

'Mr Chadwick,' I say, pulling free my Nokia and dialling up my voicemail. 'This voice. Do you recognise it?'

Chadwick presses the phone into the kink of his head, frowning darkly as the short message plays through.

'Bill O'Malley. I'm sure of it.'

'Thought so.'

'When did you receive this?'

'Just before eleven last night.'

'Christ.' Chadwick frowns. 'So at some point between being reported missing and washing up at the bottom of a cliff Bill O'Malley decides to phone you up and threaten your daughter?'

'So it would appear.'

'Which means your number will be stored on his mobile.'

'Clearly.'

'That's not like Bill, you know.' Chadwick shakes his head. 'He's a bastard, alright – *was* a bastard – but threatening *children*? Seems odd.'

'The call sounds strained to me. Maybe whoever killed him forced him to make it.'

Chadwick considers this. 'But who?'

I haven't the energy to tell him about this morning's encounter with Andre and Franck, despite my suspicions that they're connected with O'Malley's murder. The fresh mud on Andre's boots, Franck's grazed knuckles, that business on the cliff top; I've little doubt that these Gallic goons are our men. But who's buttering their croissants? That's the question.

'More bad news, I'm afraid,' says Chadwick. 'O'Malley may well have your business card on his person as well, Dark. Demanded it before he left Alfred's – said he was going to bill you for any dry cleaning to his suit. Said he'd phone the police if I didn't hand it over.'

'Great.'

'Sorry. Look, Dark, maybe we should just...'

Hand ourselves in? Let investigations run their course? Chadwick doesn't say as much, though I watch the thoughts flitting across his brow like the shadow of a passing plane about to slam nose-first into a building with both he and I in the cockpit.

'Uh huh.'

'What then?'

'We think this through.'

'Okay.' Chadwick nods, pulling back on the throttle and aiming for clearer skies, at least for now. Which is great. Because as bad as it is here at the Duke of York the lager in the holding cells at Rouge Bouillon is *appalling*.

'Can I have another listen?' Chadwick holds his hand out for my Nokia, eyebrows raised in question. I nod permission, hand it over. He presses a few buttons and holds it to his ear, lips moving soundlessly as the message repeats.

'I know where this is, Dark!' he blurts after several seconds. 'I know where they had him! That hissing you can hear in the background...it was high tide last night, yes? And that scraping sound...wood on stone, I'm sure of it. Add the echo and the fact that O'Malley's body was found where it was and I'll bet you a hundred pounds this call was made from...'

'Corbet's Folly. The tower.'

'Perhaps.' Chadwick starts suddenly as his mobile buzzes to life and starts treating him to a tinny version of Stevie Wonder's *I Just Called to Say I Love You*. 'Excuse me a moment.'

'You're that politician, right?'

Chadwick freezes, phone to ear. An old chap in a filthy suit ambles up to our table, his finger raised. Piss-yellow hair. Smell of sweat and chips. Got some horrible tattoo leaking out above the left collar.

'I seen you on the television, sheg. You're into all that green energy shite 'n that. Me wife thinks you're a *right* twat but I tell 'er you're not as bad as the rest of them. *He's not as bad as the rest of them*, I tell her. Least he cares about this bloody island. Least he cares about the coast 'n that. This place'll be another bloody Hong Kong if it weren't for blokes like you. You keep giving that Terrata lot shit, mate. You keep giving them bastards shit and that. *Fuck* what my wife says, eh?'

Chadwick recovers sufficiently to muster a few words. 'Why th...thank you. I most certainly will,' he says, shielding his phone with his hand. 'Keep giving them...um...*shit*. And that.' He turns into his phone, shielding the mouthpiece with his palm. 'Hello? Alice darling?'

'*Fuck* what my wife says,' the old man announces loudly to the room. 'Not as much of a twat as the others, this one.' He continues to jab his index finger down at the crown of Chadwick's lowered head, well after the York's assorted public have turned away.

'Sorry honey I...yes. Right.' Chadwick's frown deepens. 'And you told them I was...right. At the York. Um...'

'This one's alright,' the old man concludes, shuffling away.

'...no reason honey. No, no. Don't worry, it's nothing at all. Yes I'll be home soon. Ok. Bye.' Chadwick sets the phone down, teeth bared in the manner of a man with bad news to share. 'That was my wife. The police have been in touch. They want a word, apparently. She said that I was...um...'

'You told her you were coming here?'

'To meet a parishioner, yes...'

I'm already on my feet. Moving over to the frosted glass of the front windows I peer out into the grey. No sooner have I done so then I spy a telltale steak of neon yellow approaching from the turn of the road. Clearly we don't warrant sirens just yet, though the speed at which they've reached us suggests that the net has been cast. We're wanted men.

'Follow me.' I've time to slam back the last of my Carling before hooking an arm under Chadwick's and dragging him with me towards the toilets. There's a fire door out back through which I've staggered more than once. 'They're here.'

'But we can't...we can't just *run* from the police,' I hear Chadwick bleating behind me as we scurry down a grimly tiled corridor. 'Dark!' he calls, as I slam into the bar of the fire door, tipping us out into the rain swept alleyway beyond. 'This isn't how it's done, damn it! Where are we...what are we...oh wait for me Dark, wait for me!'

10 – Taxi For Two

This isn't how it's done, damn it. Chadwick's words cling like burrs as the taxi – a private affair, swiftly dialled – eases us away from St Helier town centre. He's right of course; it isn't. But then I spent over ten years in an office doing things the way they're done and where did *that* get me?

How it's *done*: pushing numbers round a screen; shuffling paper in your dreams; spending your days moulding piles of other peoples' cash into neat little rows for a handful of your own to take home and pat into the walls.

Not that I didn't do well out of it, for a while. Louise's mother and I had amassed a lovely little pile of our own by the time I decided to kick the whole lot down. It took me years to destroy it properly but I got there in the end; neither my ex-wife nor Dr Griffiths nor anybody else could hold back that great big foot of mine once I'd gotten started, though they tried, damn them. They tried.

But down it all came, thank god, at home and at the office, in corridor and street. And what a day that was, when this hamster finally slipped his wheel! I'm told that I made at least three of my fellow money-moulders at Staunton and Sage sob before the boys in blue turned up to drag me from the building. Served a few home truths, apparently. Threw Malcolm Carter-Reeves' framed photo of the Queen like a Frisbee, they say. Urinated across my desk. Threatened to hole-punch a vein. Rampaged around the entire second floor *like some drunken rabid monkey*, according to one witness statement. *A traumatic event for everyone involved.*

Good. Here's hoping I gave them all something to think about. Mammon's drones, the lot of them; Danny K with his beloved yellow Lamborghini, Melissa Reid of the braying laugh and golden nails, Malcolm and his precious Friday golf.

'Idiots.'

Our taxi driver is one of those dour, defeated types, his face long since melted like warmed butter over the upper curve of his steering wheel. He stares past the wipers with heavy lids, no doubt counting the hours until he can go home and ignore his wife in front of the football.

I treat him to a quick Sherlock from the back seat. Fingers of his right hand tanned with smoke, B+H, twenty five a day. Heart attack already on order from Amazon. Ate three sausages for breakfast today; couldn't finish the last one. Massive racist. Brother in Sheffield; estate agent, also hates his job. Irrational fear of bats. Nearly choked on a piece of apple when he was twelve. Left ball slightly smaller than the right. Elementary, my dear.

Okay so I'm just guessing about the sausages and the brother in Sheffield and the bats and the apple but of the rest of it I'm pretty sure. Deductive reasoning, like Chadwick said earlier. Used to be my *forte*, though I'll admit to having let it slip these past few months. I've let a lot slip, if I'm honest. These are greasy days. Even the most basic attempts at observation feel like I'm trying to make out the bottom row of a wobbly chart held up by some sadistic optician. *That's a C, that's a U, that must be an N...*

'Fucking Porkos,' mutters our driver as a white van swings

clumsily out in front of us.

See? Told you.

'I beg your pardon?' Chadwick swivels to frown over his shoulder. Fair play to the man for hanging on to his principles, even if his career, life and sanity are currently hanging by a single Labrador hair.

The taxi driver declines to comment, just mumbles something to himself and melts a little further down his steering wheel.

We're on the residential outskirts of St Helier now, heading north up the steady incline of Queens Road through corridors of bush-topped granite wall. We'd passed the Police Station on our way out of town, Chadwick and I simultaneously turning away from the window and sinking down into our seats like some bleakly choreographed dance move.

'So tell me, Mr Dark.' Now Chadwick leans in furtively, hopping aboard my train of thought. 'How the hell does someone like you end up a private investigator? Does it pay?'

'It pays. You've paid, right?'

'Like I said. I transferred seven fifty yesterday. You'll get the other half when I see some results.'

'You'll get results.'

'Hmm.' The politician chews his lower lip. 'You're not how I'd imagined a PI would be. What did you do before all this, if you don't mind me asking?'

'Marine biologist. Specialist in eels and other slimy beasts.'

'You're joking, right?'

'Of course. I hate water in all its forms.'

'An unfortunate place to be born, then.'

'Earth?'

'Jersey. An island.'

'Oh. Quite. I'd requested Mars but...hey ho.'

Mars would be nice. Just me and the Rover (NASA will have fitted it with a bottle opener, surely? Silly not to). Louise would come visit, of course. I'd set up a shuttle or something.

My eyes are closing. 'Tell me about Corbet's Folly,' I blurt in an attempt to shake off my drowsiness. 'Terrata want the site for flats, yes?'

'*Luxury* flats, Dark.'

Of course. All Terrata flats are marketed as *luxury* over here. As if possessing ceilings, doors and enough room to break into a slight jog before hitting the far wall represents the height of opulence.

'They were close to buying it, too.' Chadwick shuffles his knees towards me, giving me his full attention. 'Though not with a view of knocking it down. The tower's a listed building so they couldn't, even if they wanted to. No, the architect's plans have the tower spruced up and incorporated into a luxury residential complex. Eight circling flats with sea views. Modern design. All angles, glass and headache. You know the sort.'

'What was stopping them?'

'We were. *I* was. We'd managed to pull Terrata up on a technicality in the Island Plan, forced them to make some last minute changes to size, environmental impact, that kind of thing. Basically stalled them whilst I tried to muster as much firepower as I could in the States to get the bloody thing blocked.'

'And how close were you?'

'Nowhere near. Our only hope was...well...' The politician sighs. He turns to the window, mournfully matching the gaze of his reflection. 'Progress, Dark. It's all seen as progress. Investment. Expansion. Inviting the mega-wealthy to use our coast-line as a sun bed for two weeks of every year. And in the process the island's heritage gets steamrollered.'

'You appear to care for us *crapauds*. That's nice.'

'Look, Dark. Just because I wasn't born on Jersey doesn't mean I don't love this island. I've been here over twenty years now. And it's the bloody principal of the thing.'

'Great election platform too.'

'You'd be surprised, Dark. There are plenty of Jersey folk out there who couldn't give a stuff about their heritage. Most islanders couldn't even tell you who Moses Corbet was.'

'_____'

Chadwick snorts.

'So fill me in then. Moses Corbet.'

'You've heard of the Battle of Jersey, yes? 1781?'

'I know enough.' The surprise French invasion. The English besting their snail-gnawing invaders in the Royal Square. Major Francis Pierson taking a metal marble to the heart and having a pub named after him for his troubles. (Nice selection of ales they've got in there, though the current barmaid's got a dicky eye. All a bit awkward.)

'Moses Corbet was the island's Governor at the time. He was the one the French got out of bed having snuck up on the south east coast – around a thousand of them in all, once they'd lost a ship or two to the rocks. Shook Corbet awake around eight in the morning and insisted he hand the island over or they'd burn St Helier to the ground. Bit of a bluff, but Corbet wasn't to know that. You've got to feel sorry for the old chap. Just imagine.'

'Waking up to find a Frenchman in your bedroom? The very stuff of nightmare.'

'Surrender or we'll burn St Helier to the ground.' Chadwick shakes his head. 'Poor Moses. Some choice.'

'The choice being what colour lighter to lend them. Or flint. Or whatever they had back then.'

'You don't mean that, Dark.' Chadwick gazes out reflectively at the scrolling greenery. 'Though one suspects that Corbet ended up wishing he had. Called their bluff, that is. Instead he just gave up the ghost. Surrendered. Worse, he ordered the rest of the island militia to surrender too, which didn't sit too well with Pierson, who promptly stuck two fingers up at the French and opened fire. Took the English about twenty minutes to confiscate the Froggies' ball and that was that; one failed invasion and several hundred seriously pissed off French prisoners. Pierson died in the battle, of course, and remains a local hero to this day.'

'And Corbet?'

'Disgraced, court-marshalled and stripped of his governorship. Returned to the island a pariah, albeit one with a rather generous pension. Spent the rest of his days mooching about a disused Martello tower on the north coast of the island.'

'They gave him his own Martello Tower?'

'Not as such. The foundations of Rozel Tower – or 'Corbet's Folly' as it came to be known – were laid by a previous governor in an attempt to beef up Jersey's defences. After the

1781 fiasco it seems focus shifted to other areas of the island's coast and Rozel Tower was left unfinished. Until Corbet's return, that is. For some reason – call it guilt, warped sense of duty or plain old madness, Corbet seems to have taken it upon himself to complete the tower in order to spend the rest of his life watching out for those pesky French.'

'Making amends. Earning forgiveness.'

'Quite. Trouble was that no-one wanted anything to do with him. As such he was forced to rely on the worst of the islands' tradesmen, with the end result being...well...a slightly shitty tower. Hence the name Corbet's Folly.'

'He died there?'

'Not sure. Lived to a ripe old age though. The Folly stayed in the family for years, until one by one Corbet's lineage died off or simply disappeared. At present the tower's just kind of floating in administrative limbo. It's the States' to sell.'

'And that's where you come in.'

'That's where the National Trust comes in, yes. As does Terrata, damn them. They slipped up though, overshot with their development proposals, fell foul of the Island Plan. Lots of delicate wildlife up on the North coast that needs looking after. Can't just go pouring concrete on it all. We were on them in a flash. They'll get round it eventually though. There are more than a few slick palms in the States, though you didn't hear that here.'

'And now, after O'Malley's death?'

Chadwick winces at the mention of the dead man. Lost in the island's history he's forgotten that the pair of us remain shackled to a bloated lump of rotten Irish meat on an autopsy table not too far from here.

'I don't know, Mr Dark," he mumbles, staring out at the scrolling hedgerows. 'I just don't know.'

It's been fifteen minutes since we left the pub. Already the lager's wearing off, the lizard spines of my hangover visible beneath the waves and rising. Time to unleash the artillery, see this monster back to the depths. More booze is needed, and soon.

The dark red awning of a Costcutters looms on the left. I ask the driver to pull in.

'Need a biro,' I nod towards the shop. 'Might get some fruit too. You want anything?'

Someone's let the air out of Chadwick. Now he slumps morosely like some punctured Politician Doll™, his large forehead pressed white against the window glass.

'Hey.' Warmed to benevolence by the prospect of looming booze I lay a hand on his shoulder. 'It's going to be okay. That video of you and Scooby-Do most probably died with O'Malley. The rest we can sort. Trust me. You'll be okay.'

I step out into the rain and dart into the store. Once inside I hurry over to the sad selection of over-ripe fruit they've got rotting against the back wall. Grabbing a sorry-looking banana for cover I head back to the front of the shop where a pale assistant wilts glumly at her till. I instruct her pallid and unhappy face to pass me a half litre of vodka, a packet of Benson and Hedges and a lighter.

Having paid with a twenty slipped from Chadwick's wallet back at the Canon (expenses) I unscrew the cap from the vodka bottle as the receipt chatters from its slit. The assistant – a gaunt, haggard thing with a ring through her lip – fixes me with a glare of evident disgust.

'Diabetes,' I tell her, in between wince-inducing gulps. 'Left my insulin at home.'

'Wouldn't a chocolate bar be better?'

I shake my head at her over the lip of the bottle, its contents already halved.

'Mister you are *sick*.'

'Why thank you,' I squeak. I'm lifting an arm to wipe the sheen of Smirnoff from my chin when two teenage boys burst into the shop. One wears a hooded top, the other an Arsenal football shirt. The latter has a smart phone in his hand which he swipes whilst jabbering excitedly at his friend.

'I swear man, that's *him*,' he giggles. 'That's Kevin's dad. Watch this. Watch.'

The pair bustle past me and over to the magazine rack. Together they huddle in over their tiny screen.

'All over Facebook mate. It's Kev's dad, I swear.'

'From the TV? In the government 'n shit?'

'Yeah man yeah. I swear. Watch. Watch this.'

Having slipped the half-empty vodka bottle into my pocket I pretend to take an interest in a rack of birthday cards, all the while with an eye on the boys' faces as they fizz like twin fuses above the screen.

'Is that a...?' The hoodie cranes in closer.

'I know, man. Now watch. Watch this. I *swear* man this is *sick*...' The phone owner's voice rises, the grin on his face threatening to tear his head off at the jaw. 'Check it! Look!'

'Oh my god man oh my god oh my god!'

I leave the boys in a mushroom cloud of high and hysterical laughter and quit the shop. The rain's picked up outside. Waving my banana like some hard-won sports trophy I rejoin Chadwick in the back of the taxi.

'Onwards,' I tell our driver, 'and don't spare the horses.'

'What horses?' he grumbles darkly, indicating out into the road.

'I think I recognize one of those boys,' says Chadwick absentmindedly, glancing back towards the shop as a tiny soul band starts up in his trouser pocket. 'Goes to Kevin's school.' As he turns he hoists a buttock and reaches for his mobile, where Stevie Wonder's now in full swing.

'I wouldn't answer that,' I tell him, stilling his arm as he attempts to wriggle his mobile free. 'They'll triangulate you.'

'They'll *what*? But it's my wife.'

That's what I'm afraid of. If the video's been posted to Youtube then chances are Alice Chadwick will have been alerted to it. There may well be Hell on the end of that line.

'Trust me. You answer that phone and a big red dot appears on a screen at police HQ. Next thing it's all screeching wheels, sirens, choppers. We're wanted men, yes?'

'Well...*yes*, in a way, I suppose. Dear God can they actually *do* that over here?

'Triangulate? Easy. Anyone can do it with the right equipment. And Jersey police have the right equipment.'

A total lie, blindingly white. Chadwick gawps, stunned.

'But...Alice. I can't just...what if one of the kids is hurt or something?' He quivers, visibly buckling under the mental strain of denying his wife an immediate ear. Poor man; run one of those ultra-violet fingerprint detectors over Chadwick and I'll bet you'd see his wife's thumbprint whorling straight down over his shoulders from the crown of his head. This guy is *tamed*.

'Mr Chadwick,' I say, grabbing the door handle. 'If you answer that phone I'm gone. I refuse to be triangulated. For you, for anyone. Seriously, I'll run.'

'Not without paying you won't!' yells the cabbie over his shoulder. 'And what's all this shit about being wanted men?'

'Nothing to worry about, sir,' I call forward. 'Just rehearsing our lines for this year's Gilbert and Sullivan. Church thing.'

Chadwick has his thumb on the keypad of his mobile. One squeeze and his world – and this case – comes crashing down. If I want to find out who's threatening Louise then I need Chadwick in one relatively calm and functional piece, not some gibbering, blubbering, suicidal mess. That's *my* role.

'Give me the phone, Gary,' I urge. 'Give it to me or turn it off. At least until we've come up with a plan. Don't let them triangulate you. It's not nice.'

The two boys have emerged from the shop clutching cans of energy drink, the smart phone still between them. Things are still hysterical. *Nyuck nyuck nyuck*. Chadwick turns towards the sound of their laughter, at which the one in the Arsenal shirt makes a lunge towards the taxi, his arm raised, eyes wide in startled recognition. *Hey mister*, he calls.

And then we're off, the cabbie swinging us out and on through the leafy depths of St John.

Chadwick's phone falls silent.

'Mr Chadwick. Give it here.'

And he does, blinking hard before turning back to mope at the window with a final, heavy sigh.

The taxi accelerates down a corridor of drab granite walls and sodden foliage. The light is low and bleaching, the grey day clinging to the windows of our chariot like a grieving widow to a hearse. It's dead out there, on the Styx. Up front our driver huddles and mutters, a low grade and overweight Charon, his face dribbling slowly down the wheel.

'Sharon? Are you taking the fucking piss mate?'

Oops. Must have said that out loud.

'Yes my friend,' I reply. 'I'm taking the piss. But not out of you.'

The driver shakes his head, as around him and us and everything else the piss continues to be taken, cellular-level piss, galactic piss...all these atoms, molecules, and snickering quarks...*taking the fucking piss*, all of it, though out of whom or what I'm not so sure. Our grand and ultimate Driver perhaps, some poor omnipotent schmuck with a torn, faded map who even now is spreading his arms in celestial consternation at this pathetic mess of a planet and yelling mutely with tangible and ocean-flecked fury: *are you all taking the fucking piss mates? Are you all taking the...*

11 – The Folly of Moses Corbet

'Dark. Wake up man.'

I come round with a start. I've been out seconds, though it feels longer. Note to self: lowering of lids unadvisable. Maintenance of full consciousness at all times advised.

'Are we there yet?' I ask, massaging the vision back into my eyes.

'Yes. Look.'

I do, immediately recognising the gravel car park into which the taxi has crunched as the one to which my French goons brought me earlier this morning. Same cliff-top crumble, same sweep of sea; somewhere beyond the grey scowl of the Channel the horizon skulks behind a wall of mist.

'Twenty four pounds,' the driver barks into his rear view mirror. I leave Chadwick to sort this out – I assume he knows I'll only add it to his expenses tab if he doesn't – and step out into the cold, blowy wet. A hundred metres or so away past the car park's banked grass border I make out the stumpy granite tower observed earlier this morning. So that's Corbet's Folly. I cross the car park, peering through the bushes to take a better look.

Martello Towers aren't flash. Picture those curved, gently tapering buckets served as standard issue to kids on beaches. Picture them packed tight – the way I imagine my Louise used to do when her mother took her to the beach before we didn't take her to the beach anymore – and then upended, bucket removed.

Hey presto: one Martello Tower. Sure you need slits and crenellations and stuff from which to fire arrows into your enemies' eyes and the *real* things – like this one – are made from granite and hollow inside but essentially that's the shape.

This one's different though. This one's not been packed down very well. Or filled with enough sand. Or even filled with sand at all. This one slouches in an ungainly manner; not so much a listed building as *listing*. Several granite blocks have tumbled free from the sides leaving it pock-marked, as though blasted by some huge shotgun designed for bringing down runaway castles. The slits are more a sleepy / than a wide awake |. At some point in recent history the local Banksy has scrawled the word COCK above the doorway in white paint.

Chadwick ambles up beside me as our taxi grumbles off along the main road.

'Don't these things usually have three floors?'

'Corbet simply ran out of funds,' Chadwick shrugs. 'Just about managed to cobble the roof together and that was that.'

'Still, I like it. Dinky.'

'I'll admit it has a certain...charm. Unique, certainly. Terrata's plan was to circle it with flats, offer it up as a kind of communal centrepiece. With a few renovations. And minus that graffiti, of course.'

We file through a gap in the grass bank and set off towards the tower, which sits in the centre of a field-sized patch of unkempt land a hundred metres or so away from the brambled cliff top. The sky continues to spit, a chill, needling rain that threatens to sober me up, even though the moisture is welcome to my lips. I let Chadwick get a few paces ahead of me, risking a few more swigs from the vodka bottle as he tramps on towards the tower.

'Dark! Look.'

I've just slipped the little bottle back into my pocket when Chadwick turns and waves me over to the patch of grass where he's hunkered down. He holds up a pair of men's reading glasses. Expensive looking. Got the words Hugo Boss written down one arm.

'These were just lying here.'

'O'Malley wears glasses?'

'Occasionally. Not sure if these are his though, but still...'

'And now your fingerprints are all over them.'

'Damn it,' says Chadwick, dropping his prize.

'Rain'll wash them off. Come on.'

Chadwick nods, before continuing on over the rough, uneven ground towards the tower. I manage one more surreptitious swig of vodka, pausing to stoop and collect the glasses from the grass on my way past.

Hugo Boss. A sudden recollection flares, though just as quickly it has gone again. Hugo Boss. I wait for my brain to deliver the goods but it just shrugs back, slack-jawed and empty-handed. I pick on towards the tower, pocketing the glasses and conscious of the wet grass beginning to soak into the bottom of my trouser legs. I bend, rolling them both to the knee.

At some point the tower has been ringed with wire; nearby a bright yellow sign bearing the unfinished haiku DANGER – UNSAFE BUILDING has been planted on a pole. Now both wire and sign lie discarded amidst the undergrowth.

Access to the tower is via a white wooden door set some

three or four feet above the ground, itself accessed by a rusting metal staircase bolted loosely to the brickwork. The steps shudder perilously as Chadwick clomps up, causing me to pause for fear our joint weight causes them to crumble completely.

'Let's see now.' Chadwick gives the tower door a shove. No sooner has he done so then my eyes are drawn to a flash of colour along the main road. I turn to watch as a familiar red Renault enters the car park at speed with two men in the front; moments later and a silver Porsche purrs casually in behind. From here (and with a hand pressed over my left eye) I can just make out a flash of long blonde hair in the driver's seat.

'Bingo,' shouts Chadwick, finally shunting the door open with his shoulder. 'Wasn't locked, just stiff. Come on up.'

The two cars have crunched to a stop, their bodywork discernible through the foliage separating the field from the car park. The blunt clunk of car doors being slammed carries across the grass. I don't think we've been seen yet, but that's about to change. We've got seconds.

There's nowhere to go but up into the tower. I reach for the railing, hauling myself heavily up the metal steps towards the open door, suddenly conscious of the throb at the bridge of my nose where Andre head-butted it earlier.

That sudden lurch up the stairs has left me nauseous. I belch, tasting cauliflower, bile and vodka.

'Bloody hell Dark!' calls Chadwick, his voice echoing from within the tower. 'Come and have a look at this.'

'Grrrk,' I mumble, stepping in.

12 – Towering

'They had him here, Dark. I'd put money on it.'

Chadwick's voice rolls around the circular stone interior. The ceiling is low and comes close to sweeping his hair as he strides the five or six metres across its diameter. There's not much of note; a wooden chair against the far wall, some plastic cans containing an amber liquid, a few scattered rags. At the centre of the chamber a stone staircase spirals wildly up to the next level. The light is dim, and creeps in through five wonky window slits spread unevenly around the tower's circumference. A multitude of mosses and moulds have been enjoying themselves here for some time, and in one spot a particularly determined bush has nuzzled its way in through the walls.

'Petrol,' I wince, detecting an acid tang amidst the vegetable damp.

'Must be what's in those containers,' says Chadwick. 'And look here.' He points at the chair, where ragged strips of silver duct tape have been wrapped round and then torn from the two front legs. The rest of the roll lies discarded nearby.

'This must be where they sat him, yes? And on the floor here. Is that...was that..?'

'Blood,' I mutter, peering out of a window slit. From our elevated position I'm afforded a better position of the trouser-suited blonde sliding out of the Porsche. Two familiarly lumpish figures have climbed from the Renault, and now Andre and Franck come stomping across the field, their faces set stern. Behind them the woman follows at a slower pace, her high-heeled boots disagreeing with the uneven muddy ground. Despite the wide sunglasses obscuring the top half her face I recognise her instantly as the woman from Ledger's video, O'Malley's lunch partner of yesterday. The broad forehead, the blonde, swept back hair, that distinctive Roman nose.

Already the Frenchmen have halved the distance between the car park and the tower. We've got seconds.

'Mr Chadwick. We've got company. Bad company.'

'Who?'

There's no time to explain. Grabbing him by the arm I drag him over towards the spiral staircase, shooing him upwards. From outside the tower comes the clang of boots on metal steps. I give Chadwick's bony backside a shove.

'Move.'

The steps corkscrew up towards a trapdoor that I assume leads out on to the roof. Unwilling to risk the creak of its hinges I usher Chadwick out on to the second floor. The ceiling here is lower, forcing him into the beginnings of a stoop. Being a circular room there's no nooks or corners to hide behind, though there's something resembling a crumpled up kitchen lino over by a section of the wall. It'll have to do.

'Here,' I whisper, gesturing for Chadwick to join me as I creep in to lie belly down beneath the lino's musty folds. 'Chadwick,' I hiss. 'Under *here*.'

Bloody politicians. Always know best. Peeping out from my cover I watch as Chadwick dismisses me with a wave of the hand and instead crouches down a few feet from the staircase, his big head tipped like a jug towards the voices below.

'*Really?*' The woman's voice is sharp, and drips scorn. 'You didn't think to get rid of the chair, no?'

'We forget, *madam*.' Andre's voice curls in barely concealed amusement. 'We take it now.'

'And what's with the petrol? This a French thing?'

'Mr Shah just said to frighten him. Didn't say how. Petrol best way, is how we do it in past. Is...how you say...our 'mark of trade.''

'Trademark.'

'Yes.'

'He fucking shit himself.' This from Franck, the human rat. 'Boo hoo hoo.'

Chadwick has perceptibly paled. He turns slowly to meet my gaze, body frozen, hands trembling. I place my index finger upon my lips, at which he gives an almost imperceptible nod.

'It worked,' continues Andre. 'He agree to do what Mr Shah say. Make call to other guy on his phone. Say he going to do his daughter. Now when police find his phone...*paf*.'

'Hardly conclusive evidence, is it?'

'We hang the *putain* off cliff earlier. Left him at scene of crime. Chuck some of his clothes in bushes. Plus like you said he seen having fight with O'Malley in restaurant yesterday. Is motive.'

'He is up the shit,' pipes Franck.

'*In* the shit, you mean. Jesus.' Brice paces the room, high heels clacking on the stone floor. 'I didn't agree to any of this.'

'Mademoiselle. We just follow orders.'

'Whatever.' There's a light clicking sound, the snick of something metallic.

'Ms Brice. I don't think smoking a good idea. The petrol.'

'I'll smoke where I fucking well *want*.' Brice exhales loudly. 'Just get rid of that chair, shift those containers and make sure there's nothing left from your little party last night. Okay?'

'Yes Ms Brice.'

'This has gone too far.'

'Tell that to Mr Shah.'

'Oh don't you worry. I will.'

The door creaks below, followed by the clang of heels on metal as Brice makes her exit from the tower. Then silence, broken only by the low mutterings of the two Frenchmen.

'*Salope*,' says Andre. Franck titters to himself.

Chadwick's remained a terrified waxwork of himself at the top of the staircase throughout all this, trembling with the effort of maintaining his silent stance.

I lower my head to my chin, taking careful not to rustle the lino.

From down below comes the sound of movement. A swish, a bang. Laughter. Over by the staircase Chadwick blurs, splits in two. The world begins to fade.

No. Stop.

Lowering of lids unadvisable. Maintenance of full consciousness at all times advised. And yet it's almost comfortable here beneath this lino, despite the thugs below and the sudden heaviness of my limbs and...

Stop. I jerk my eyes open, rolling them round the uneven stone curve of the tower's interior in an attempt to stay awake.

Is this where Moses Corbet slept? Imagine living out your days in this damp and lonely place. I picture the old pariah gazing out from his slits at the Channel beyond, keeping one rheumy eye open (at least keep one eye open) for those pesky French with Pierson's ghost forever blowing insults over his shoulder...

Surrender!

Cold metal jabs me in the forehead. I awake to find myself staring up along the length of a barrel, beyond which lurks a dark figure, its shadowy features indistinct yet terrifying.

Suddenly the darkness parts to reveal a Cheshire cat grin, an ice-white crescent of teeth.

Surrender, Mr Dark. The island is ours.

I swipe at the musket – because no, I will not surrender – only for it to pull back beyond my reach. I struggle up, but rough hands shove me back on to my bed. A peal of cruel laughter rings out and now I feel a pressure on my chest; something heavy is squatting there, pinning me down. A bullfrog. There's a huge brown bullfrog on my chest, its fat throat swollen into an obscene balloon, its dense weight crushing the breath from me.

The bullfrog winks and suddenly the musket starts to gush a thick amber fluid...because it's no longer a musket but a beer tap I'm staring up into, and those are no longer sights but a vertical handle, a brown hand pulling the pump down and now I'm drowning, suddenly I'm going under like my...

I jerk gasping into the underside of the lino. It takes me a moment to remember where I am, to realise that Chadwick's mobile is buzzing furiously in my back pocket.

Andre. Franck. They'll hear it. Pushing back the musty folds of my cover as quietly as I can I reach around for the phone. The buzzing – accompanied all the while by Mr Wonder and his band – has stopped before I manage to wriggle it free.

How long have I been asleep? And where's Chadwick gone? He's no longer crouched at the top of the stairs.

More buzzing, though no song this time. A text message.

ANSWER ME FOR FUCK'S SAKE GARY

Groggy and with vision swimming I thumb through the phone's recent history. There are two more messages behind it and an equal number of missed calls. All from Chadwick's wife.

JUST SEEN IT. PHONE ME NOW, reads one. The other simply says DOG?

Wriggling free of the lino I make it on to all fours, taking care to mute the curses and grunts that threaten to pop from my parched lips. Another glance around the room, just to make sure I'm not imagining things.

No sign of Chadwick.

And then comes laughter from below:

'Pauvre bébé, pauvre bébé!'

I grimace to my feet, my limbs leaded. From below comes a shrill scream, its echo curling round the walls. Then the sound of something being slapped. Then a whimper.

Found him.

Fighting nausea I tiptoe over to the top of the stone staircase, resting a steadying hand upon the central spoke as I lean in for a better look. The air is thick with the stench of petrol, and from below comes the splash of liquid on stone.

'Please...god...no!' It's Chadwick's voice for sure, though cracked and shrill with terror.

Moving as quietly as my stiff limbs and dizzy brain allow I begin to descend the spiral stairs, craning my head around the curve in an attempt to see what the Frenchmen are doing to my client. Inch by inch I go, edging slowly down into an acrid fug of petrol fumes and the unfolding horror below.

13 – Inferno

'You ever burn to death before, *putain*?'

'You not got so much fat to burn but you tall. Like big candle. Hey, Franck?'

'Gonna burrrrn, baby.'

'And when you finished burning we sweep you up and bury you. No-one know where dog-fucking politician gone. Maybe he just kill himself he so ashamed he got caught fucking a dog.'

'You fucked a dawwg, baby. You fucked a *daawwg*.'

'Maybe we leave your clothes on the beach and people think you swim off and drown.'

'And then the fishies fuck you man, yeah! The fishies *fu-uck you maaa-aan*.'

Ever seen a Frenchman miming somebody making love to a shoal of fish? I hadn't until now, but there Franck is, frantically pumping the air with his groin. Run Nemo, *run*.

It's official. Things aren't looking too good for Gary Chadwick. The Frenchmen have bound him to the chair with duct tape; ankles to the chair legs, arms in a tight V behind his back. Every last inch of him has been doused in petrol, from the clumps of hair clinging to the bulge of his forehead down to those ridiculous camouflage pants, now soaked and clinging to his legs. I watch on, still hidden by the curve of the staircase as Andre lifts one of the two plastic containers and sloshes the last of it over Chadwick's wailing head.

'P...please! No!'

With the silent grace of a panther I somersault into the fray, dispatching Andre with a karate chop to the side of the neck and locking both knees around Franck's head. The Frenchman struggles but already it's game over; a final squeeze of my thighs and his head explodes like a melon, showering us all in brain pulp. Chadwick high-fives me as I free him and we head swiftly off to the nearest pub for a pint. Chadwick buys.

Meanwhile in *this* reality I watch on trembling as Franck slaps a length of duct tape over Chadwick's mouth.

'That shut you up,' he sneers.

It's then that Chadwick spots me, his eyes bulging wildly as they skid up over the Frenchman's shoulder to catch me loitering behind the pillar. I gesture him to hush, yet in raising a finger to my lips I lose my balance, staggering down the last few steps and out into the open with a frustratingly audible curse.

The Frenchmen spin.

'You!' barks Andre.

'Monsieur Smelly,' sneers Franck.

Oh for a lobster to hurl. In that longed-for parallel universe where his steaming brains lie splattered I'm a brutal killing machine; here in this one my martial arts skills are marginally less than zero. The only black belt I can seriously lay claim to is the ring of scum round the rim of my bath. Running is pointless (as well as a physically impossible) as is retreating back up the stairs. As is *anything*, come to that, though now is not the time for philosophy.

Already I'm smelling Spirigel and that faint odour of warmed rubber that permeates the intensive care unit of the General Hospital. They've admitted me a few times over the past two years; at least this time I'll have someone else to blame for the damage.

Interesting. My brain's already waving a white flag though it appears that my arm, hand and mouth have other ideas.

'Two Frenchmen,' I find myself babbling, ramming Chadwick's phone against the side of my head. 'First one's called Andre. Six one. Skinhead. Scar on forehead though may just be a zip. Barbed wire tattoo round neck.'

It's a bluff, of course. I'm talking to an empty line, though hopefully this will make them think twice before committing themselves to anything drastic like setting Chadwick alight. This is a small island, after all, should they find themselves wanted men. Limited egress. Tight borders. Ish.

Franck takes a step towards me.

'Second one's shorter,' I blurt. 'Franck something. Man-rat. Corbet's Folly, right now. Red Renault Clio. There's a Mr Shah here as well.'

'Motherfucker!' blurts Franck.

Mmmmphh! struggles Chadwick.

I shrug at Andre. *Let him go*, I mouth, nodding at their kindled prize.

Andre and Franck swap anxious glances. Not the brightest flip-tops in the carry out, these two.

'Actually officer, I think it's probably best if you...'

My words trail off as the mobile starts fizzing yet another tinny rendition of *I Just Called To Say I Love You*. Ten out of ten to Alice Chadwick for persistence.

The Frenchmen's eyes narrow at the sound.

'Sorry officer.' I roll my thumb across the keypad, stopping Stevie in his tracks. 'Don't know what happened there,' I continue, as a wife-bomb explodes in my ear:

'Gary for fuck's sake what's going on I've been trying to call you all morning there's this fucking video of you Gary with your dick up a fucking dog and I'm trying my best to keep the kids from hearing about it but they're bound –'

...and then Andre is lunging for me, fists swinging, teeth bared. I manage to duck the first few punches, though within seconds he has me by the scruff of the neck, hauling me down level with his knees. Fresh toecap is about to be served, and cold. I swing a fist into the Frenchman's groin; a devastating move, were it not for the fact that I possess all the punching power of a magically animated teddy bear.

I'm down in the petrol puddle now, my clothes quickly soaking up the fuel. Toecap is duly served, though I manage to get my palms to it (ouch), before it connects with my head. I roll, Chadwick's phone dropping from my hand and clattering across the stone floor. I slam my lower leg up into the back of Andre's, buckling him at the knee. He drops. I roll again, colliding with the second plastic petrol container and knocking it over on to its side. Petrol spouts across the flagstones, *glug glug glug*. Reaching over I grab the container, lifting it high so that fresh petrol gushes over Andre's back and legs.

'Non!' Andre shoves me away in an attempt to avoid being doused further, allowing me time to scramble wonkily on to my feet. The empty vodka bottle has tumbled loose; I shatter it with a stamp of my foot, sweeping up the sharded nozzle with my free hand and waving it wildly at the Frenchmen.

Mmmmmph! Mmmph! Throughout the melee the legs of Chadwick's chair have been clattering an untidy tap dance over the stones and continue to do so as he tries unsuccessfully to wriggle free.

'Motherfucker!' Andre stares down angrily at his wet arms, the sodden front of his t-shirt. Like the rest of us he's soaked in petrol, a pool of which shimmers slick across the stone floor. The rising fumes are intense, cloying. A wave of dizziness hits me. The room blurs though my focus is swiftly sharpened by the green cigarette lighter Andre has pulled from his jacket pocket.

'Andre!' says Franck. 'Vous etes *foux*?'

'He's not crazy,' I say, dropping the petrol container and pulling my own cigarette lighter (little orange one, real cute) from my trouser pocket. '*Me*, however – I'm nuts! *Clinically*. Ask Dr Griffiths. Ask my wife. Ask Mr Chadwick here.' I hold the lighter out at arm's length, my thumb resting lightly on the flint-wheel.

Silence descends, broken only by the tiny splats of petrol dripping from our sodden clothes.

Andre glances at Franck, whose face has frozen in the horrified rictus of a man in the midst of some deeply unpleasant underpant malfunction. Chadwick's mumblings have ceased, his wide eyes joining Franck's for a horrified dance between the two cigarette lighters.

'Okay,' says Andre, slowly lowering his lighter and tucking it back into the pocket of his jeans. He raises his palms. 'Okay then mister. Easy now.'

'Untape him.'

'Franck. The mouth.'

Franck moves over to Chadwick, his tiptoed attempts to sidestep the petrol puddles reminiscent of the overdone creep of a pantomime villain. (I took her once, at her mother's insistence, I took her to the...)

"AHH!" The tape tears free from Chadwick's jaw. *'Jesus, Dark! What are you doing?'* he shrieks. The upper part of his face is puffed with tears, giving it the appearance and texture of over-ripened fruit. 'Put that lighter down or we'll all go up!'

'What happened? How did they get you?'

'I sneezed. Couldn't help it...they heard me. They didn't spot you under that carpet, I didn't tell them you....'

'Lino.'

'Lino, carpet, whatever! Get me out of here, man!'

Andre is planning a take-down; I can see him tensing, knees set, fingers curling. I swing the lighter in a tight arc towards him.

'Woah there.' Andre raises his palms. Franck's found a little island of dry flagstone upon which he's doing a funny little one-legged dance. Won't save him; there's enough petrol vapour in the air to incinerate us all should I flick the wheel.

'I'll do it!' I shout. 'God help me I'll do it. We'll all go up! Oblivion has its attractions, yes? And I'd like French Fries with mine.'

I find that last line funnier than I probably should.

'Either of you ever been married?' I ask, slowly waving the lighter from left to right, my thumb resting carefully on the wheel. 'Children?'

'Non.'

'I have. Wife, daughter, house, home...had it all. Great job, too. Great friends, great everything. Mr Two-Point-Four, that was me. Had it *all*.'

'Congratulations, monsieur.' Andre gives the smallest of bows. 'A lovely story. Now put the lighter *down*.'

It's moving of its own volition now, that little orange lighter, dancing from Andre to Franck, from left to right and for a second I'm elsewhere...it's Louise's fourth birthday again and there's cake, a big Peppa Pig cake, with candles, and I'm stood outside in the playground looking in through the windows of the community centre where the party's being held, and the approaching police cars have turned their sirens off at my ex-wife's request but still the kiddies have got their little faces pressed to the windows, tiny mouths making little Os on the glass as they watch the funny man setting fire to newspapers in the playground, because I just want to light Louise's cake for her, I just want to light my daughter's cake like this and this and...

'Put. It. Down.' Andre has taken a step closer, palms raised. 'You had it all, monsieur. We hear you...'

'But what I also had was *this*.' My arm is moving of its own volition again, lifting the remains of the vodka bottle and tapping it lightly against my head. 'What I also had was this *brain*. This condition. It's genetic, you know? Passed down from one generation to the next. Like a vase. Like a really, really *bad* vase.'

My heart's thumping in my chest. Muscles tensing.

I don't feel right.

Andre holds up a hand. 'This is great, really, *mais ecoutez...*'

'No!' I yell, surprised at the volume of my own voice. Because suddenly it occurs to me: what do these guys really know about *my* story, what I've been through, where I've *been*?

Does *anyone* know? Does anyone actually *care*? And why won't they let me light my daughter's cake?

Something bursts within me. *Houston we have a problem.* Full system malfunction. Steam ruptures, needles spin wildly, internal klaxons sound. My cheeks are suddenly hot with tears and my voice has gone all high and whiny the way it does when the pipes burst, which they've been known to do on occasion, which they just have, and I don't feel right, I don't feel right at all.

'*You* listen!' I roar, at once one with and witness to this blubbing angry torn-up puppet version of myself – with that lighter dancing round in the air before me as though it's alive, like some plastic flinted imp – observing from afar yet conscious of the pulsing of my veins, the movement of my jaws, the rough jag of the metal wheel against the pad of my thumb.

'I didn't ask for this!' screams puppet-me, whipping frantic at its strings. 'This fucking time bomb in my head! All those years carrying a time bomb round in your skull, tick tick tick tick here's your wife and tick tick tick tick tick here's a child and tick tick tick tick here's your home and are you happy now, are you happy now, 'cos HERE I GO! BOOOOOOOOM!'

The Frenchmen retreat with palms raised as I advance towards them, hysterical, scarlet, bellowing. 'YOU KNOW WHAT IT'S *LIKE* TO HAVE A BLACK HOLE IN YOUR HEAD? YOU KNOW WHAT IT'S LIKE TO HAVE A FUCKING *WORMHOLE* IN YOUR HEAD? EITHER OF YOU TWO GOT A WORMHOLE IN YOUR HEAD?'

'Monsieur, please...the lighter...'

'Dark, calm down, for god's sake please calm down...'

'NO I WON'T CALM DOWN!' I hear myself screaming from afar, 'NO I WON'T CALM DOWN AND THERE'S NOTHING THAT CAN CALM ME DOWN BECAUSE I'VE GOT A WORMHOLE IN MY HEAD AND NO MEDITATION NO COUNSELLING NO ANGER MANAGEMENT NO RESIDENTIAL PLACEMENT NO NONE OF THAT FUCKING SHIT WORKS WHEN YOU HAVE A BLACK HOLE IN YOUR FUCKING HEAD AND IT ALL MEANS SHIT IT ALL MEANS FUCKING NOTHING IT ALL MEANS SHIT YOU'RE BORN YOU SUFFER YOU LOSE IT ALL AND DIE ALONE SO WHAT'S THE POINT OF ALL THIS...THIS FUCKING...THIS FUCKING...'

And then suddenly I'm down on my knees – the marionette tumbling, strings snipped – my world becoming once more a wall of petrol-soaked flagstones, the pink spread of fingers splayed and grasping, a spool of spit unwinding from my lower lip. Oh look, look at those little bits of moss and lichen peeking out from the cracks in the stone! Have I frightened them with my wailing? No – their tiny fungal arms are extended in sympathy; *there there, giant crying monkey, it's alright*, even as my sobs continue to reverberate around the stone walls of the tower. *It's alright.*

Murmuring softly I claw at the cracks with my fingernails, peeling free a little clump of lichen, just to keep in my pocket, just to keep as a friend, just for the company. *It's alright, you weeping stinky ape*, says my little moss buddy. *Let it all out.*

I think

I think I need help.

'You okay, man?'

The little one with the ratty face. Franck. I feel his hand on my shoulder, tentative at first, then firmer. How good of him to care. Only I know that the real reason for Franck's concern is the little orange plastic thing in my hand. That thing with the tiny metal wheel that could still roll us all to hell with the merest flick of my thumb.

'Come on man. *Allez*. Up.'

I do what Franck says, rising slowly to my feet, shrugging his hand free from my shoulder. I watch the rise and fall of his breathing, see the terror in his eyes, the beads of sweat on his brow. Behind him Andre remains frozen, palms raised, brow knit with panic.

I am the judge. I am the jury. I am the executioner.

And I know what I must do.

'Burn him.'

Chadwick's lower lip tumbles as though it's suddenly come unstuck from his face. A whimper escapes him. I raise the lighter – on which my thumb remains primed – so that it is level with his eyes.

'Politicians,' I spit. 'Self-serving scum. Hypocrites, the lot. I say we burn them all. Starting here.'

'D...Dark, man,' he bleats. 'What are you *doing*? My children! My wife! I've got...'

'They'll live, Chadwick. They'll live. No-one wants a dog-fucker for a dad, anyway.'

'Monsieur Dark.' Andre nods, his relief palpable. 'Come on.' He nods towards the door. 'Out we go. Then like you say...' He mimes a big fiery *whoosh*. 'We do it.'

'Marigold, p...*please*.' Chadwick tries desperately to wriggle his arms free, but the duct tape holds fast. 'Please, I beg you...

'Hypocrites!' I yell, spitting at his feet.

'Liars!' blurts Franck, beginning to enjoy himself anew. 'I like this guy, man,' he says, giving me a thumbs up. 'I *like* you.'

'Sorry Gary. Looks like you misjudged me.' Reaching for the roll of tape I silence Chadwick's sobs by tearing off a fresh strip and slapping it over the lower part of his face. 'I'm going to make sure they play that video at your funeral,' I murmur, leaning in close to his ear. 'The vicar's going to *hit the roof*.'

Having planted a farewell kiss on his forehead I turn away and head for the exit with the Frenchmen. Andre's picked up the petrol container, with which he scatters a rough trail of petrol in our wake. Pausing briefly at the door I take a final glance at the condemned man slumped head-bowed and shuddering in his chair. He doesn't look up as I wave farewell. Think I may have upset him.

Oh well. Eggs and omelettes.

Andre, Franck and I step out of the tower, clomping down the metal staircase and on to the grass. To my dismay the rain has thinned; conscious of the petrol on my clothes and skin I run my right hand along the wet railing as I descend, taking care to wash what I can from my fingers.

'All yours,' says Andre, offering up the staircase with a sweep of his arm. He pulls off his petrol-soaked shirt, baring his thick, tattooed torso to the elements. Swastikas, flags and fists ripple as he twirls the shirt into a makeshift fuse before laying it over the top step, which still drips slick with the last of the petrol.

Andre's dark eyes sparkle. A mean grin splits his lips. He

steps back to join Franck a few metres away from the tower, the better to outrun a human fireball should one come screaming his way.

I lift the lighter so that it is an inch or so away from the end of the twirled shirt. Keeping my arm in this position and my thumb on the flint wheel I turn back to the two men.

'Last night. This morning. You paid Yola to trap me, yes? So this Mr Shah of yours could frame me for O'Malley's murder.'

'You trap yourself when you turn up yesterday asking questions at the hotel, monsieur.' Andre folds his arms. 'Yola just keep you close until Mr Shah work out what to do with you. Now *do it*.'

'This Mr Shah. Who is he?'

'He the man who pay us,' the Frenchman shrugs. '*C'est tout*.'

'So you're Mr Shah's bitches?'

'We're no-one's bitches,' Franck snarls. 'We come to this shitty island because he pays us well. Back home we...'

'Ta bouche!' Andre gives Franck a silencing shove.

'Setting Chadwick up with that dog not enough? Shah actually wants him dead? Like this?'

My arm is beginning to ache but I keep the lighter held to the fuse, my thumb simultaneously massaging the wheel and holding their focus.

'This bit just fun,' says Andre. 'We get rid of body afterwards – take it out in Mr Shah's boat and dump it – everyone will think he kill himself because everyone see him with dick up dog. Now *do it*.'

'And me? I end up framed for O'Malley's murder?'

'We see.' Andre shrugs. 'I think maybe Mr Shah have you

wrong. I think maybe he have work for you.' He nods at the lighter in my hand. 'Mr Shah is *trop cher*. Very rich man. Billions. He soon to be big dick on this island. Useful friend to have.'

'Mr Shah gonna fuck this island.' Franck grins, grinding his pelvis once more. His special move, clearly. 'He gonna fu-uh-uh...'

'Mr Dark,' glares Andre, his eyes narrowing. 'The lighter, please. *Do it.*'

I look down at the cute little orange lighter in my hand.

I look up, scanning the empty sky for a sign.

Orange lighter.

Empty sky.

Orange lighter.

Long enough.

Click.

A spark is all it takes to send a thin spine of blue flame racing up the twirled shirt. Arriving at the petrol-puddled step the fire blooms with an audible *whoomph* before racing in and over the doorstep of the tower.

There's a flash and a dull crump as the petrol-fumed air of the tower's interior catches light. Orange flames spurt from the window slits, blue tongues lapping at the edges of the door. The blaze is instantaneous.

I stand there, arms shielding my face against the heat. Andre nods approvingly. Franck begins to dance and holler. He's doing that thing with his pelvis again.

14 – Driving Test

Never was a big fan of fireworks. Standing round in the cold staring up at expensive sky-sized screensavers just never did it for me. I could get much the same view sat at my computer desk with a bottle of wine, if I wanted (which I didn't), far from all those inane *ooh*s and affected *aah*s, and with nary a cinnamon stick in sight.

Still, I took Louise to one, once. Her mother made me. One of my more socially conscious in-laws had organised a big do in an unused field outside their needlessly massive house somewhere in the wilds of Trinity. Some charity affair, money going to the homeless or the autistic or cerebral palsy or something nice and smug like that. Rattling tins, raffle prizes and runny noses, that sort of thing.

Not that Louise cared much for the charity side of it. She was just there to watch things burn up and explode. *Look Daddy look*, she'd gasped, pointing up as the sunless sky filled with burning metal salt. *So pwetty! Like fwowers!* Her ankles had wriggled within the stirrups of my elbows; I remember wondering at the glorious weight of her little body on my shoulders, the cold crunch of her anorak against the back of my neck.

Later, as we'd stood staring with the crowd into a big pile of burning wooden pallets I'd told her all about brave Guy Fawkes and his followers. How they'd set about trying to kill the king because he believed in a different imaginary being to the imaginary being that Guy Fawkes and his men believed in. How they'd plotted to blow up the Houses of Parliament with gunpowder. How they'd failed. How they'd been punished by being strangled half to death before having their willies cut off and burnt in front of them because it's what the King's imaginary God would have wanted. How they'd then had their intestines pulled out through cuts made in their stomachs whilst they were still alive. How Guy Fawkes had escaped this bit by cleverly snapping his own neck at the gallows. Hurrah for Guy Fawkes!

It was only after I'd bent down to light Louise's sparkler that I'd realised she was crying. She was never a wailer, my Louise – unlike her Dad – but instead had this way of simply lowering her head and quietly emptying her eyes. A functional, almost pragmatic approach to crying, quite unlike the screeching, hysterical lamentations favoured by her hideous bitch-cow of a mother.

I'd apologised for scaring her, told her that it was all just a joke, that Guy Fawkes had actually lived to be an old and happy man, before treating her to a lemonade and another pint of mulled wine for myself, returning sheepishly for the lemonade (and another mulled wine) which I somehow managed to forget to buy again, twice. Shortly after that a dodgy rocket went off in someone's face and the ambulance got called. The bowl of mulled wine got stolen during the hubbub; the rest I forget. I think Louise was taken from me (or 'found wandering' as some local drama queen later phrased it) by one of her mother's friends and returned home, whilst I came to several hours later in a sick-spattered drainage ditch minus my shoes and with a cinnamon stick wedged firmly up each nostril.

Here in the grim wet drizzling Now the show's coming to an end. The middle floor of Corbet's Folly burns for around a minute (*look Daddy look!*) and then after that there is only smoke, burnt air and the occasional wisp of smouldering straw floating clear from the open doorway.

'He fucking did it, man!' guffaws Franck, pointing a trembling hand at me. 'He kill him! Oh man! This guy is craaaazy!'

Andre slowly nods his agreement. I spy a newfound respect for me casually swinging its legs upon that Neanderthal brow ridge of his. He sets on up the steaming stairs, cuffing me lightly on the shoulder as he goes. Franck follows, giggling to himself. I linger at the bottom, staring up past the tower's crenellations at the sky for a sign, some indication of what I should do next.

Andre disappears into the smoking belly of the tower, arms raised to his face against the remaining heat. Franck completes his clump up the metal stairs and follows him in.

With the men gone I begin to back slowly away from the tower towards the car park, scanning its roof for signs of movement. Tense seconds tick by. My stomach flutters horribly.

Come on, Chadders. I'm halfway across the field now, closer to the car park then the tower. The angle between myself and the roof thins. Still nothing.

I've just killed a man.

My stomach bucks. Fist to mouth I feel a rush of bile rising, though nothing comes. My arms are shaking.

I've just burnt my client alive. I've just...

'Dark!'

And then a familiarly bedraggled figure rears up into the sky, bursting above the tower's crenellations like some cut-price jack-in-the-box. It's him.

'Chadwick!' I hiss, waving. 'Quick!'

A younger man could probably drop the distance safely – Corbet's dwarf tower is a mere twenty foot or so in height – but instead my client begins a clumsy descent, lowering himself down by way of the cracks and footholds that stud the uneven wall. Chadwick's no Spiderman but he's getting there.

'C'est *quoi*...?'

An angry shout echoes round the interior of the tower. I'm guessing Andre's staring down at that charred, empty chair and wondering who cancelled his order of *flambéed* politician to go. Maybe he's staring at the sharded remains of the vodka bottle that I slipped into Chadwick's bound hands when I whispered *hit the roof* into his ear.

'Quick!'

Chadwick drops with anchor-like grace to the base of the tower and starts speed-hobbling towards me across the field. I'm metres from the car park now, eying the Frenchmen's car and praying that they've left it unlocked. A key in the ignition and a decent CD in the player would be nice as well.

'Chadwick! Over here!' I'm guessing Andre and Franck will be raging around the second floor right about now, kicking that old lino around, staring up through the open trapdoor at a huge middle finger the shape and bleary hue of the sky.

Chadwick's bust his ankle during dismount. No matter. On

he stumbles, his clothes sodden and clinging, face a wet and bloodied mess, strips of roughly shorn duct tape trailing from his ankles.

'Wait for me Dark...wait!'

Having cleared the grass bank I bear down on the Renault, resisting the urge to kiss its roof upon finding the doors unlocked. No ignition keys though, damn it. I'll worry about the CD player later.

Turning back to Corbet's Folly I spot a furious faced Andre pointing over at us from the roof. A volley of Gallic invective fires over the field. Games's up. Clock's ticking. There are thirty seconds between myself and Andre's steel toecaps, maybe less.

When was the last time I tried hotwiring a car? Ah yes, nearly five years ago, whilst halfway through Christmas dinner at my sister-in-law's house (I'd have made it as well if the red of my party hat hadn't caught my ex-wife's eye through the kitchen window). Granted I'm less drunk now though this time I'm performing under considerable pressure and with the continuing rigidity of my skeletal frame at stake.

Think man, think. I pull out my Swiss army knife, prise the ignition cover free with its tiny blade.

The passenger door is wrenched open. Chadwick hurls himself into the seat in a cloud of panic and petrol vapour. 'Hurry, Dark!' he shrieks, dark snot blasting from his nose. 'Get us out of here!'

I glance across the field towards Corbet's Folly. Franck has already made it to ground zero and is scurrying across the field towards us. Behind him Andre bursts from the tower, vaulting over the side of the stairs and landing on the grass in an animal crouch.

Ignition cover off. Leads everywhere.

Red ones, yellow ones.

Pretty leads. Nice leads.

'You can do this?' blubbers Chadwick. 'You know how to do this?'

Battery leads. Starter leads. What do you do again, cut them? Rub them together? Which ones?

'Um,' I say.

'FOR GOD'S SAKE DARK DO IT!' screams Chadwick, slapping the dashboard as the Frenchmen tear across the field. Franck's pulling something from his pocket as he runs; behind him Andre is closing the distance in great strides, arms pumping the air like a hundred metre runner, the sinews of his upper body taut, his nose wrinkled, his teeth bared.

'Lock your door! The button, Gary!'

Franck is the first to hit the side of the car, slamming hard into Chadwick's window with his elbow. The car rocks though the glass holds.

Chadwick screams, his big head colliding with mine as he backs away.

'Mr Chadwick. *Please.*'

'Gonna fuck you maaan!' Franck's spittle blasts the glass. Behind him Andre vaults over the grass bank and cop-rolls over the Renault's bonnet to join me on the driver's side.

'YOU FUCKING DEAD!' he screams through my window, frenziedly slashing his own throat with a finger. 'JE VOUS TUE!' Meanwhile Franck's found a fist-sized stone which he lobs at the windscreen, instantly cracking the glass.

The fractured web holds in its frame, though I've a good feeling the next rock's coming through.

Toecap o'clock.

Over on the passenger seat Chadwick's gone foetal. It occurs to me that our looming slaughter means that I won't have to tell him about his recently acquired Youtube fame. Should put an end to this bloody headache of mine as well. Silver linings, as Dr Griffiths used to say. *Pays to stay positive.*

Wires in my hand. Red and yellow.

I look down at the Swiss army knife, trying to recall which of these little silver edges is the screwdriver. That one. Slipping my thumbnail into the slit I pull it free from its housing just as Andre pulls a Bruce Lee with his size elevens, shattering my driver's door window completely. Glass explodes into the car; only a last minute feint from myself prevents his boot from connecting with the side of my head.

'MOTHERFUCKER!'

Draining the last drop of beer from the final bottle in the emergency cellar at the Last Chance Saloon I jam the screwdriver blade as far as it will go into the ignition. Twist. Twist again. The car wheezes. Clutch down. Twist again. Andre's fingers tear at my throat. Car comes to life. Chadwick screaming. First gear. Throat being squeezed now. Accelerate. Handbrake. Accelerate. Throat still being squeezed. Andre's hot breath as he attempts to bite my face. Accelerating now, spinning the steering wheel hard right. Andre no longer trying to bite my face. Throat no longer being squeezed. Horrible bump as rear right wheel goes over something solid.

Stop. Reverse. Another bump. Chadwick still screaming.

'GOGOGOGOGOGO!'

With one final jerk of the gearstick I hammer the car forward and we shoot off across the gravel towards the car park's exit. In my rear view mirror I see Andre on the ground, clutching a leg that is no longer the shape a leg should be. Franck's giving chase but we're gone, we're gone...

'GOGOGOJESUSDARKGOGOGO!'

Screeching out on to the main road I hurl the wheel left and gun the Renault into third, whooping with delight as the engine picks up its roar. We're tearing along the length of the field now, drawing momentarily level with Corbet's tower which I swear – I *swear* – tips us a slow and approving nod as we pass. Raising an arm through the shattered window I give it a thumbs-up in return, screaming my goodbyes in the rear view mirror as the mist draws its curtains and the Folly is lost from sight.

15 – Stuff

'We need y'in, Dark. I cannae help you otherwise. The press have got wind of O'Malley's death 'n Chadwick's name is being thrown about. Both of you – come in or we'll come get you. *I'll come get you.*'

Ledger's putting on his Hollywood voice. There's a movie playing in his head, a movie in which the Glaswegian is the commanding spoke of a busy crisis centre surrounded by stern, gum-chewing FBI times staring intently into live feed monitors. Multi-angle CCTV stills of Yours Truly fill a room-length screen on the wall. Jerky lenses peck at worried faces, flit over grimly furrowed brows. Cigarettes smoulder. People are saying 'goddammit!' a lot. There's black coffee everywhere. All eyes are on Ledger as the anxious grunt trying to trace my location looks up from his computer, gesticulates to keep me on the line, keep him on the line...

'Are you in the toilet, Iain?'

'Now what in *fuck* makes you say that?'

'I can hear the cistern filling behind you. You taking a number two?'

'Of course I'm nae fucking...' Ledger quietens to an angry hiss. 'I was passing the bogs when you rang, as it happens. I'm not supposed to be talking to...well you know the bloody score. Saw your number, jumped straight into this cubicle and found myself staring down at a pot of last night's fuckin' stew. My lucky day. Flushed then answered. Swapped one turd for another.'

'You could have just lowered the lid.'

'It would still have been *there*, Dark. *Waiting*. For Christ's sake,' he snaps. 'Why are we talkin' about another man's *shite*?'

'It's thanks to another man's shite that I'm out here, Iain. I'm being framed. Made an accessory of. Me and Gary Chadwick. Someone's trying to link us to O'Malley's murder.'

'You did a pretty good job of that yourself. You and that lobster of yours. Waking up half naked at the murder scene won't have helped your defence much either.'

'I didn't wake up there, Iain. I was dumped.'

'Whatever. It isn't me you need to be telling this to. Blake's in charge of this one so it's him you'll need to -'

'No way.'

I'm leaning against a bus shelter a couple hundred metres or so down from the Silverwood retirement home. Nice area, this. Expensive houses with pools, couple of campsites, some slick hotels. The main road is broad, its gutters gurgling. Traffic is thin. Chadwick's still hunched over the dashboard, his head in his hands. He's said little since our escape from the tower, piping up only to weakly enquire why I was driving with a hand over one eye. I'd been too busy trying to pick out the road through the shattered windscreen to respond. He didn't touch his can of Strongbow (we found two in the glove compartment) so I had that too. Something to settle the nerves; we've been through a lot.

Not sure I should be stood out in the open like this but the car needs an airing and I need a break. My hands are shaking, the petrol vapours are making my guts churn and my mouth's so dry I just spent half a minute licking rain-water from the

Clio's roof runnels.

'Not a good look, Dark.' Ledger's scowl is audible through the pain. 'Running like this. The actions of a guilty bastard, if y'ask me.'

My moustachioed friend has a point. Us running away like this is going to look real bad if we get nabbed. At the same time I'm not prepared to spend the next forty-eight hours playing bad cop bad cop in a tiny room with Chief Officer Arnold Blake and his men. *No way Jose*. There are things that need sorting. People to see. Cracks to fill.

'I'll be in touch, Iain. Give my love to Jan. You make a lovely couple.'

I leave Ledger furiously barking my name, pocket my phone and wander back over to the car.

'Dark.' Chadwick's long head peeks out from the open window as I approach. He speaks softly, his voice barely carrying through the idle thrumming of the Renault's engine. 'What now?'

A fair question. We can't keep driving round in this smashed up car. Granted I'm only a minor celebrity amongst the local force but several years in local politics has rendered Chadwick's face unmistakable. If we're spotted and stopped, we're *done*. We need cover. Cover and a bottle or two of Merlot. Maybe two. It *is* lunchtime, after all.

Time to call in a favour.

Leaving Chadwick to his misery I amble back over to the cover of the bus shelter. Pulling out my mobile I bring up the Farmer's number and press call.

As usual his phone rings straight through to a message

recorded some time around the close of the last decade. *Hi there*, purrs a woman's voice, like something out of an advert for high-end chocolate. *You've reached the de Gruchy residence. We're not here right now, but go ahead and leave your number and we'll get back to you when we can. Thanks.*

'It's Dark. I'm on my way. Red car, one male passenger. Long story.'

I hang up.

We're not here right now.

You can say that again, Abigail.

Last time I laid eyes on the owner of that voice she was having her mainbrace spliced doggy-style on the deck of a gleaming white yacht anchored a mile off the coast of St Peter Port, Guernsey. The yacht's owner, a barrel-chested Cypriot named Costos Blowkoski, had somehow picked me and my long distance Canon EF out on the horizon and waved – pausing his assault on Abigail's *derriere* long enough for an actual, definite *wave* – before returning to his task with a bay-spanning grin and a triumphant punch of the air.

As well he might. A real looker, Abigail de Gruchy. Like something that fell out of a magazine. I could see why Jean was prepared to pay me good money to track her down. I picture her now, all blonde curls and dark sunglasses, pouting down from the throne of her Land Rover, a stream of cigarette smoke blown high and thin. Abigail was Jean's second wife, (cancer having chewed up the first), twelve years his junior, uneasy stepmother to his three sturdy sons and certified gold digger, last spied in the process of having her tanned, Lipo-sculpted posterior repeatedly skewered by my cheery Cypriot friend.

144

None of this got back to Jean, of course. And even if it had – even if I'd presented the Farmer with the photos – the irrefutable proofs of Abigail's infidelity would merely have popped like bubbles against the dome of his delusion. Stubbornness is a singular trait of all *crapauds*, though the trauma of having yet another wife vanish on him seemed to have elevated Jean de Gruchy's to a higher order. Like some over-bearing bodyguard his brain had long since tricked his mind into believing that Abigail's disappearance was all part of an island-wide conspiracy involving senior members of a rival farming family – the Ricous – a conniving, blackmailing and (according to Jean) paedophilic lot who had wormed their way into positions of power within the island's government and who were now set on establishing a farming monopoly in which the de Gruchys were to play no part.

But of course. It all made sense to Jean. The Ricous had his wife. Locked away in a barn somewhere, kept alive via a diet of grain, cow piss and onions and awaiting god knows what fate. His princess in a tower. Poor Abigail.

Worse, there was nothing Jean could do about it. The Farmer's version of reality had Ricous snipers roaming the lanes of St Peter and St Mary with orders to blow his balls off the minute he set foot outside the parish border (literally his *balls*, hence his continued insistence on wearing a small metal jockstrap fashioned out of an old biscuit tin and some string). This fear of having his gonads sniped, coupled with Jean's peculiar form of parish-based agoraphobia (his last jaunt outside of St Ouen having occurred in 1994, whilst high on home grown mushrooms, having spied JC himself waving at him from a distant phone mast) meant that the chances of the Farmer personally scaling the walls of Abigail's imagined tower were significantly less than zero. And this pained him daily and made him drink huge amounts of calvados.

All nonsense, of course. The Ricous – a shrinking and rather innocuous clan of St Martin tomato growers – were no more involved in political conspiracy and hostage taking than I was. The Farmer's three massive sons Oscar, Jed and Devlin were well aware of this, though had long since grown used to humouring the old man. They'd hired me less out of care than curiosity; more to make sure that Abigail was gone for good than out of any real desire to get her (and the credit cards, and the Land Rover etc etc) back.

And so it was that when Costas Blowkoski, Cypriot haircare magnate and owner of the thirty foot *Silver Dolphin* raised his hand and waved across the bay I'd simply packed up my camera and booked myself in on the next flight home, pausing only to accidentally drink myself into a three day stupor from which I emerged face down in a stranger's tent on the neighbouring island of Herm.

Professional to the last I'd still had the pen drive on (or rather, *up*) my person; the photographs, the flight details, and (most damning of all) a CD containing twenty five minutes of taped and rather ugly telephone talk between Abigail and her new millionaire boyfriend, in which Jean was variously referred to as 'pee-wee,' 'maggot dick' and 'that foul old bastard.'

All of this was handed over to eldest son Oscar in return for my fees up front and a promise to keep my discovery to myself. As far as Jean was to be concerned the Ricous had Abbie, and would continue to have her to such time as they didn't, whenever that might be. Oscar had even had me mock up a phone-tap intercept of two unidentified Ricous discussing Abigail's transferral to an unknown – though tastefully furnished – bunker in the soily depths of Grouville, the better to console poor old Jean.

Quite safe, I'd had the rascals confide in each other. *Misses her old man but knows he's coming for her one day. Insists on keeping herself trim downstairs just in case he bursts through the door. Costing us a bloody fortune in Immac. Proper mark of love, that is. Admirable in a woman. Twice we've caught her trying to carve his name into her breast with a sharpened hairpin.*

Okay so I'd run away with the script a little, but the actors had played their parts well enough to cause Jean's shoulders to crumple upon first hearing.

'My poor baby,' he'd crooned, stroking the plastic pate of the CD player, with Oscar's paw laid reassuringly on his shoulder. 'The boys will come for you one day, my girl. Just you hang in there. She's keeping her fanny smooth, Dark. Locked up alone at the ends of the earth yet still keeping her fanny smooth for her old man. Caged like a modern day Persephone and still buffing her minge. My dear, brave girl...'

'I'm going to be sick again!' yells Chadwick. And there he goes, leaning out the window of the battered Renault and unspooling something thin and yellow, which is duly escorted by the rainwater to the drain.

'My phone,' he gasps, wiping his mouth with a sleeve. 'I need to call Alice.'

'Your phone is now a tiny plastic Frisbee welded to the floor of Corbet's Tower, Mr Chadwick. I'll go back later on and scrape it up if you want, but for now...'

'I need to call...I need...'

'You're okay, Gary. You made it out.'

'Did I?' Chadwick snaps, chin slick, hair plastered wildly across his forehead. '*Did I*? They were going to burn me alive, Dark. They were going to...I thought you were going to let them...'

'Mr Chadwick. Chadders. Please. I need time to think.'

I roll my burning forehead against the cool perspex of the bus shelter, trying to ignore the chemical bailiff hammering at my door. Those Strongbows barely touched the sides; I need something more substantial to kick this hangover into touch. There's an off-license across the road, though something tells me Chadwick's not in the mood for a carry out.

No. No more booze, not just yet. I need what little wit I've left about me to get a grip on this. Time to figure out what's going on with this Shah character, find out what he wants. There's got to be a way to extricate myself, Chadwick and – most importantly – my daughter from this mess.

Something's been niggling me since I picked up those Hugo Boss sunglasses back at the tower. Something fat, dead and Irish is waving at me from behind the curtains of consciousness, if only I can find the drawstring. Something I've missed.

Returning to my Nokia I scroll through my message inbox. Nothing since a reminder text from my dentist last Tuesday; I doubt that she's involved. I check my call log instead, finding a call made to my mobile at 14.04 yesterday lunchtime. The number's unknown to me, yet there it is again at 22.54 last night – that threat to Louise – from the very same mobile number.

Bill O'Malley's number. Looks like he phoned me yesterday, just thirty minutes or so after our spat at Alfred's. The conversation length racks in at just under two minutes.

Hmm.

Something swells, bursts. A bubble of recollection, words and images swirling vaguely in its sheen.

I need to see you, Mr Dark. Blue walls. A thick wooden table, atop which a sheaf of paper, those Hugo Boss glasses. O'Malley's face, the sweat running off him. *There's something I need you to look into for me. It's urgent.*

The vision is fleeting, but it's enough.

I've a feeling that I met up with Bill O'Malley yesterday afternoon. I think he gave me something. I think he needed my help.

'Er...Dark?'

I peel my face from the bus stop and turn back to the car, where Chadwick is waving me over under the pretence of patting down his hair. Having caught my attention he bears his teeth, rolling his eyes over at the police car pulling in to the bus bay where we've stopped.

Damn it.

Having positioned his vehicle diagonally across the front of the Renault the officer climbs leisurely from his seat. Leaning against the side of his door he regards our battered ride with a bemused air, thumbs hooked into the loops of his neon jacket.

'Gentlemen,' nods six-foot-something of Rouge Bouillon's finest beef, his Judge Dredd jaw jutting out beneath the lowered visor of his cap. A whopper, this one; in terms of human grammar this guy's a full-stop. Our time with the Renault ends here. It's been a blast.

'Is this your vehicle, sir?' The officer catches me tracking back along the pavement with as much nonchalance as my semi-inebriate petrol-pocked brain will allow.

'In a manner of speaking, yes.'

'And the windscreen, sir?'

'Ours too.'

'I'm afraid I can't let you proceed any further with it, Sir.' The officer tips his head back, black eyes glistening. The deference is a game; I can see he's playing me as a cat would a wounded mouse. Probably got a semi just thinking about the sound the side of my head's going to make when he slams it down on to the bonnet.

'Who says I've been driving?'

'Officer.' Chadwick extends a handshake, promptly ignored. 'Not sure if you know who I am but...'

'Have you been drinking, Sir?'

'Yes,' I reply, feeling the usual lemming instincts rise. 'Consciously, constantly and consistently for about the past eight or nine years. You?'

The officer unhooks his thumbs, hands gliding slowly down to his sides as though lowered by invisible strings. Somewhere in the ether an unheard harmonica gives a plaintive Western wail.

The officer's eyes narrow. His tone hardens.

'I'm afraid I'm going to have to ask you to accompany me to the station for a breath test. Sir.'

'Who says I've been driving?'

'He's been driving,' blurts Chadwick. 'Sorry Dark but you're not making a bloody liar of me. You're alright though, yes? You've only had the one beer earlier and that er...cider...um.' He falls silent, flinching.

'This pen-knife, Sir,' calls the officer from the driver's side. 'The one rammed into the ignition. Yours?'

'Yes. And I have the receipt, before you ask.'

The officer reaches through the remains of the shattered window and gives the knife a twist. Two weak chugs and the car falls silent, as though in response to an embarrassingly bad joke.

'Right sir,' says the officer, with a concluding air. 'Here's how it is. I'm arresting you on suspicion of driving a stolen vehicle...'

'...I prefer the word *donated*, but if...'

'...of suspicion of driving whilst under the influence...'

'...driving? Who said anything about dri...'

'...and, very shortly, with resisting arrest. Please step into the squad car, Mr Dark. You too, Mr Chadwick.'

A bus is approaching us along the main road, its bald driver's face already scrunched in indignation as he spies the clog-up in his bay. There's no way he's making good on his indicators' promise, so instead he pulls up a few feet behind the police car. The bus deflates a little, as though giving voice to its master's despair. The officer, Chadwick and myself turn to watch as a geriatric conga line begins to make its way down the steps.

Perhaps I should consider taking one of the old folks hostage. That old man with the stick looks skinny enough to drag or hoist up over my shoulder, though where I'd run to I'm not quite sure. The old folks' home down the road, I guess. I can think of worse places to hold a siege; biscuits and board games galore plus someone's bound to have some gin stashed somewhere.

'Stay right where you are please, Sir,' barks the officer, as if sensing my intent.

Having dribbled its passengers out on to the pavement the bus sucks in its gut and sets off past us, though not before Chadwick has attracted the attention of a young couple towards the rear. Youtubers, I'm guessing, fresh from their latest Facebook update; for upon having the politician pointed out to her the girl's eyes widen in the manner of a child on a Disney ride (Canine-Sodomists of the Caribbean, It's a Dog's World, something like that). He says something funny. She bites her lower lip.

Luckily Chadwick's too preoccupied with his own mounting misery to note the advent of his recently acquired fame. At the officer's insistence he's folding himself into the back of the police car, his long legs forced vertical against the back of the driver's seat so that his chin rests almost on his knees. From here he glares out at me like some awkwardly packed mannequin as the door slams firmly on his face.

No thanks. I'm out of here.

I'm gone diddly-on.

Shoving myself clear from the side of the police car I lunge for the back of the bus as it sweeps by. The plan is to place a foot on the corner of its bumper, grab a hold of its rear window wipers and be whisked clear to fence-jumping / undergrowth-scurrying / manhole-squeezing distance before Officer Dribble has time to react.

That's the plan. The reality of the move is somewhat different, due to the absence of a) wipers and b) a bumper. Instead I effect what could best be described as a failed hug of the vehicle's back end, culminating in a hastily arranged three way conference call between myself, gravity and the tarmac.

'Shall we be going, Sir?' The police officer stands above me, his sarcasm spilling like the contents of a cracked egg over the back of my head.

Enough. It's time I got out of here. Anonymity be damned; what's the point of having superpowers if you have to keep them to yourself? No-one's going to believe these two anyway when they report what they saw.

Nutters, they'll say.

As if.

'Have it your way,' I mutter. Holding a mental image of the Duke of York's interior tightly in my mind (same table, different stool) I instruct myself to jump. Time freezes; space warps as I teleport out of there, leaving Chadwick and the officer gaping at the empty alcoholic-shaped imprint on the road.

Have it, non-believers!

16 – Tick, Glock

'Not even for a second?'

'For God's sake, man. Give it a rest.'

'Denial, Chadwick. Dangerous thing. Admit what you saw.'

'I saw what *he* saw.' Chadwick nods up towards the police officer – one Officer Howe, according to the ID card on the dashboard. We're all snug in the back of his car now, being toddled off back to the station to play the usual games with plastic tubes and fingerprint ink and all that stuff.

'Which was?'

'A sad lunatic lying face down in the road.'

'I'm not a lunatic, Mr Chadwick.'

'You bloody well are.'

'Seriously though. I disappeared for a second, didn't I? Just a flicker.'

'Officer? Can you drive a little faster please?'

Mont Les Vaux unfolds as we curve our way beneath a tunnel of trees towards the pub-speckled snug of St Aubin's harbour. Giving up on Chadwick I turn instead to the scenery in time to watch The Shell Garden gliding by on our left, with its row upon row of shellfish stuck to borders, walks and walls. One of the island's more unique tourist attractions, back when Jersey had tourists; one could spend a morning pointing at the various crustaceous remains embedded in the architecture, and then an afternoon down at the Nazi-built War Tunnels picking out the remnants of Polish POWs embedded in the walls. Happy days.

'For sale,' I mutter, noting the sign as it flashes by. 'All for sale.'

Bye-bye then, Shell Garden. It'll probably end up in the hands of some international financier, its cockles, mussel and ormer shells chipped off and replaced with fifty pence pieces, the rest simply scattered with chunks of chrome and glass. I'd fashion something similar using bottle tops and wine corks, if I had a garden. Or a house.

'I'd roll the window down if I were you,' says Chadwick, leaning forward to catch Howe's ear. 'They doused me in petrol, you know. I must reek of it.'

And he does. Not that Howe seems all that interested – hasn't said a word since slamming the car door on us – though once or twice I've caught his eyes on my face in the rear view mirror, dark, inscrutable, humourless.

Something's bothering me. Something isn't quite right about this latest little arrest of ours.

'I say officer?' Chadwick tries again. 'Could you possibly let a little air in?'

My eyes snag on the dimmed display of Howe's radio. There's been no contact with base since our arrest. Or before it, come to that. None of the usual police band jabber.

'I'm afraid until I can change these clothes I'm...'

Come to think of it, I don't recall being read my rights, either.

'...matter of safety...'

And he knew our names. He already knew our names. *Please step into the squad car, Mr Dark. You too, Mr Chadwick.*

I give the door handle a sly tug, ready to run the risk with a rolling belt of fast-moving tarmac if I have to. Locked.

'...of course I'll be giving a full statement to your superiors...'

Think we're in trouble here; time to call in the cavalry. Affecting a yawn I reach slowly into my trouser pocket for my Nokia, though no sooner do I have it fingered than I feel the cold glare of the officer's eyes upon me in the rear view mirror.

Hidden in the tumble of my lap my thumb traces the distant landscape of my keypad. A tiny buzz reminds me there's a password needed. I fumble blindly. That's the asterisk, right? That must be *nine*, that the *seven*. So this button here is *zero*?

Holding Howe's gaze in the mirror with a painted grin I fail the unlock code once, twice, the mobile throwing a brief buzzing fit both times.

I've got one more chance before it freezes me out. Come on, damn it. Why didn't I just opt for 0000 as an unlock code, like everyone else? But no, I had to be clever and go for 0001 instead.

'...absolute thugs, the pair of them...'

Success. That all-important digit finds its home. I'm in.

We're halted in traffic. Something on the passenger seat has drawn Howe's attention; he reaches over, distracting him long enough for me to slip the Nokia from my pocket and risk a glance down at the screen.

Calls. Contacts. *De Gruchy*.

'...identifying them should be...'

'Shut the fuck up.' Howe grips a Glock pistol in his right hand. Its snub nose pokes out between the front seats, twitching from Chadwick to myself as though sniffing out which one to shoot first. 'Just *shut up*.'

The muzzle comes to rest in line with my left temple. As ever when staring down the barrel of a gun (because yes it's happened before) I find myself experiencing an odd sort of vertigo. That urge to swipe at its bearer, the near-intoxicating pull of oblivion; part of me aches for the blast, the finalising slam of metal through bone.

'May I?' I ask, reaching forward.

Falsely assuming that I mean to disarm him Howe cracks the gun into the side of my head. Chadwick yelps. The shock of the strike knocks my mobile from my left hand; having thudded lightly against the top of my shoe it disappears under the back of Howe's chair.

Balls.

'Next time it's a bullet in the knee,' says Howe. The clipped, professional tone from earlier is gone, replaced with something a little more West London and altogether less charming. 'You even think about reaching for that phone again and it's a bullet in the knee. Fiddle with that door? Bullet in the knee. No more dicking around until I drop you off to Mr Shah. Understand?'

'I understand. You have a thing for knees.'

'And you seem to have a thing for wheelchairs.' Howe angles the Glock downwards at my leg. 'I'm serious. No more bullshit.'

'Bullshit fader down,' I say, spreading my palms. 'We're all yours.'

Howe turns back to the wheel. Moments later and we make the turning in to St Aubin, the road passing a smattering of shops and cafes at the base of the hill before opening out on to the marina. Tide is high, the white yachts lifting on its grey, watery palm as though ready for inspection. Off to our right a run of pubs and restaurants run parallel to the railings of the harbour wall; to the left, across a neatly cobbled expanse, stands the trim taupe and terracotta Lego facade of the Salle Paroissiale. What few pedestrians there are scurry hurriedly from awning to awning, shop to car, anorak hoods pulled tight against the rain, umbrellas held high.

Over in the corner of the marina sits the Boat House restaurant and bar, where I first met Louise's mother whilst smoking on the outside terrace. Our office parties had overlapped. *Could I borrow your Santa hat?* she'd asked, stumbling over. But there's no such thing as Santa, I'd replied. *What's that on your head then?* Just a hat. *Can I borrow your hat then please?* No, I'm pretending to be Santa.

And so on.

Despite its role in the ruination of my existence I've always loved St Aubin's harbour, rain or shine. Unlike the rest of the island the developers have yet to get their hooks into it, yet to bomb it into submission with concrete and glass. There's time, I guess, but for now it's as good a place as any to die. I decide to make a run for it the moment that I'm able.

'Mr Shah's yacht is over there.' We've parked up on the square outside the Parish Hall. Now Howe gestures over to the far end of the marina. 'He's asked me to bring you two twats to him, which is what I'm going to do.'

Chadwick nods mutely as I plan my escape route. Around the back of the Boat House or out into the road?

'And don't think about running,' Howe continues, addressing us in the rear view mirror. 'Or I get to indulge that knee fetish of mine. Maybe not in full public view, but trust me it'll happen. This gun. Your fucking knee. Right?'

Whatever. Road it is. The minute this uniformed goon lets us out of his car I'm pegging it, Glock or not.

Howe swivels in his seat, treating us to another view of the pistol's snout. 'Chin up though fellas. Mr Shah told me to tell you that *The Sabre*'s bar is open and the first one's on him.'

'*Hassan* Shah?' Chadwick frowns. 'The businessman?'

'*Mister* Shah to you.'

'But I didn't think Muslims drank.'

'This one does. Wait until you see his whiskey collection. Now move.'

'And if we refuse?' Chadwick's voice barely breaks above a whisper.

'Then I'll shoot you myself!' I yell. 'To *The Sabre*!'

17 – Looking Glass

My name is Marigold Dark. I'm an alcoholic, and a damned good one at that. I'm big. I'm bold. None of this denial nonsense – assorted flasks stashed cleverly around the house, miniature bottles hidden in the cistern, elaborate tailoring of concealed tube and wine-bag combos – no, I've always made sure to confess with relish when caught, wearing my guilt like a badge. Denial is for the weak, the ashamed, whereas I wave my alcoholism like a flag. Come see.

Since I lost my family, my friends, my job, my self-respect and my daughter it's all I've had to hang on to. Because the booze didn't abandon me like they did, didn't scramble for the exits when things got tough. The booze stuck around.

And I'm grateful; along with my private investigating it gives me something with which to differentiate the days, a means of defining myself as a man. Without it I'd be lost. Lost and *bored*, I should add. Because being a dedicated, bona-fide *professional* booze-hound opens doors, my friends. Alcohol gets things *done*.

Take today, for instance. Had I not been an Elite level, card-carrying alcoholic I'd probably be sat in some grotty pub right now staring at some dreary faraway football match on an oversized screen, clutching some half empty pint of watery pish and feeling very dead indeed.

Instead, here I am – very much alive – having been kidnapped, assaulted and then loaded at gunpoint on to a floating palace to guzzle obscenely expensive spirits with a mad Arab millionaire. And it's not even four o'clock in the afternoon.

Take note, kids. Life's all about the choices you make.

Speaking of which, I've got a tricky one before me.

Whiskey or rum? I've a bottle in each hand, both full, both bearing faded, elaborate labels. I raise them to the light, marvelling at their virgin beauty; that crisp shimmering amber, that deep sunset red. Which first?

'The whiskey's a Macallan 1939, Mr Dark. Ten thousand US dollars a bottle. Best served in ivory rimmed glasses with ice-cubes made from the tears of a freshly slaughtered toddler. But I jest, of course.'

Mr Shah grins like a bullfrog in a fly factory. Grins like a bullfrog because he actually resembles one; sleek round head, jowls that spill over the collar of his white silk shirt, eyes set deep into the brown flesh of his face. He has the obligatory rich man's pullover draped over his shoulder, sleeves lightly tied across his chest in the usual obligatory way.

I'm guessing Shah's somewhere in his late forties, though it's hard to tell with these types; cash has a habit of pushing back the years. The skin of his face is impossibly smooth. I'll bet every pore of his face has its own personal exfoliator, some nubile young Swede with a tiny micro-towel sat in a hangar somewhere just waiting to be jetted in for a buff. His greased hair is swept back in coal black ridges so dark they seem to eat the light around him in a kind of anti-halo. The rings, the gold chain necklace and matching incisor; Shah's wealth isn't so much ostentatious as self-parodic. I'm dying to kick him in the balls, but then there's Howe, the Glock and all this glorious, glorious booze.

'The rum's Angostura. Legacy, a limited run, twenty five K a pop. Not a huge fan of it myself – tastes like the devil's piss, in fact – but should *The Sabre* be unlucky enough to encounter pirates on her journey...well you get my drift. Ho ho ho and all that jazz.'

'Jazz pirates. The worst kind.'

'Take your pick, Mr Dark.'

'I feel like Alice.'

'Alice?'

Mr Shah looks over at Howe, who shrugs. Our friendly neighbourhood rogue officer is leaning against a black marble sideboard with his arms folded. We're a few steps down from the yacht's deck amidst the gleaming chrome and white leather of the kitchen galley. Chadwick's slumped where he's been shoved, tucked in tight behind the corner table and still reeking of petrol and despair. I'm on my feet, for now.

'As in Wonderland.'

'Ah. Lewis Carroll. I see.'

'Drink the whiskey...'

'And you turn into a bipolar alcoholic with a knack of getting in peoples' way.' Shah grins at Howe, who snorts.

'Drink the rum...?'

'The same.'

'You appear to have the mark of me.'

'I've done my homework. Your Facebook page is quite revealing.'

'I don't have a Facebook page.'

'Which is why your Facebook page is quite revealing.' Shah's dark eyes sparkle. 'So many lovely pictures of that cute little daughter of yours.'

His words hit me like a gut punch. I clench my teeth, focusing on the whiskey's golden shimmer as a wave of panic breaks across my chest.

'Join us for a tipple, Officer Howe?'

Howe shakes his head. 'Pass. Still got work to do. Abandoned car to bring in. Some joy-riders made a right mess of it. Windscreen gone. Petrol all over the seats.'

Shah sighs. 'Most probably blood in the boot, as well.' The bottles make tiny suction noises as he tugs them free from my palms. 'Back in my country such...*vandals* would be hunted down and punished accordingly,' he smiles, filling a wide crystal glass with whiskey. 'Public flogging. A lopped limb, even. We aren't as forgiving as you Westerners,' he chuckles, handing me my drink. 'We murder sexual deviants, by the way, Mr Chadwick, so count yourself lucky you're still alive. This is on me, Mr Dark. *Shucram.*'

The glass is empty before it's even in my hand. Whiskey roars down my throat like a burning train through a tunnel of straw. I buck, coughing, fist to mouth. Wow.

'I'm no deviant,' mutters Chadwick, looking up from his funk.

'No? I'm aware of you Channel Islanders' fondness for cattle and other beasts of the field but surely...buggering dogs is still considered deviant here, yes?'

'You son of a...'

'Gentlemen.'

The voice comes from behind me. I turn as a sharply suited blonde enters clutching some sort of electronic tablet in her hand. It's O'Malley's dining companion, Franck and Andre's overseer from the tower. One slick looking lady; hair clipped tightly back from her broad forehead, bright white collar tips breaking the dark navy of her outfit like the dorsal fins of circling sharks. Nodding curtly to Shah she steps down into the galley.

'Mr Dark. Mr Chadwick,' grins Shah, gesturing to the newcomer. 'Allow me to introduce you to Bella Brice. Bella's my eyes, ears and – occasionally – *claws* on this marvellous island of yours. As trust managers go, Ms Brice is the best, isn't that right?'

'I like to think so.' Her smile quickly fades. 'We do what we can for our clients,' she says icily.

'And that includes murder?' blurts Chadwick, hands splayed on the table before him as he attempts to rise to his feet.

'Easy.' Howe's Glock flashes, its nozzle quickly sniffing out the politician's face and forcing him back into his seat.

'I have no idea what you mean, Mr Chadwick,' says Brice coolly, without looking up from the screen of her tablet. 'And I'm not sure I care much for the accusation. Please be careful.'

'It's alright, Ms Brice,' says Shah, pulling a small metal cylinder from his pocket and putting it to his lips. 'Mr Chadwick here is having a bad day,' he smiles, exhaling a cloud of cherry-flavoured vapour. 'It appears he and Mr Dark ran into some rather...unsavoury types earlier on up at our tower.'

Brice flinches, her fingers falling still upon the tablet's screen. 'Is that so? And what exactly were they doing up there?'

'Listening,' says Chadwick, raising his chin in defiance. 'We heard you and those French animals discussing what they did with O'Malley.'

'You heard me from all the way up there, did you?' Brice looks up, her expression impassive, impermeable. 'What remarkable ears you must have. I spent the morning in town with friends. *Good* friends, I should add. *Reliable* friends,' she concludes, with the merest hint of a wink. *So fuck you.*

'Not bad, these things.' Shah holds up his electric cigarette. 'Not a patch on the hookahs of home, eh, Ms Brice? Remember the ones we shared in the Koobah Lounge? Purely business, of course, Mr Chadwick,' he smiles. 'As much as I love this island of yours there are times when Bella and her friends must come to me in Dubai. In fact there are times I positively insist! And as for you hearing her this morning up at my tower...perhaps you and Mr Dark been...you know...'

Shah glugs from an imaginary hip flask, sways a little on his feet. Cute.

'It's not *your* tower.' Chadwick speaks slowly, his jaw set tight.

'But it *will* be,' says Shah. 'I want it, you see? *I want that spot.* I've fallen in love with this island!' he exclaims, spreading his arms. 'Oh beautiful Jersey! Your beaches, your bays, your quaintly cobbled streets. Your shellfish! Your sea!'

'Our competitive tax structures,' I mumble, glancing over at the sideboard where the Macallan is flirting with me. Rude to ask?

'Taxes! Pah! Cynic! As if money is all that there is!' says Shah, following my gaze. 'I *shit* money, Mr Dark!' he exclaims, reaching for the bottle and topping up my glass. 'Positively shit the stuff! This island is more to me than *money*!'

'Agreed. Our potatoes are second to none.'

'Ha! Your dinky little potatoes are only part of it! Has familiarity dulled you to the island's charms? Your French road signs. Your cows. Your slapstick government. Your obsession with the German Occupation. Honesty boxes. Bergerac! Such an odd little cultural corner, yes? Such a funny little...*niche* you Jersey folk occupy in the world.'

Wow. And I thought *I* had mental problems.

'So you think we're cute, then. Big Arab in love with a little British island. Lucky you. Cheers.' I raise my glass before sending the whiskey singing down my gullet, soaring through my veins.

Shah gives his forehead a meaty slap.

'Ha! You still don't get it! It's not your *culture* I'm in love with; it's the *erosion* that stokes these fires of mine. Such an alluring cocktail of glass and granite, money and mud! The sly, creeping stretch of capital, the way your leaders prostrate themselves to the super-rich, noses held to the stink of wealth as it smothers your traditions, your history – this *excites* me Mr Dark. It makes me hard' (clutching his nuts here, firmly in fist) 'to see the way your island is headed. Back home the deal is done – it's all over – we're on our third pack of post-fuck cigarettes! Witness the stubs glinting against the Dubai skyline – the dirham-charred splendor of Abu Dhabi – the gods of money have had their wicked way! But here, my friend, here on this beautiful little rock of yours the struggle goes on! Valiant men like Mr Chadwick here, standing up for their coastline,' (hands on hips, voice deepened in a parody of pious rage) 'for your listed buildings, your fading traditions, men who rise like plywood wind turbines in the face of the corporate hurricane that *does not give a fuck* and just *keeps on coming.* This *excites* me, Mr Dark. This makes my sap rise. I want a front row seat high above your island as it is obliterated by an atom bomb of foreign wealth. And that seat shall be atop Corbet's Tower, whether you like it or not!'

Shah concludes his speech by raising his hands into mock paws, tucking his head into his shoulders and barking wildly in Chadwick's face. Bella Brice keeps her eyes lowered to her tablet. Howe shuffles awkwardly.

'Interesting bedfellows you've been keeping,' mutters Chadwick, his eyes on the officer.

'And you'd know about bedfellows!' snorts Shah. 'Woof woof! I'm sorry about that, truly I am. We had no other choice. I can't change this island's laws, as much as I'd like to. You and your little group of lobbyists were throwing a Labrador-sized spanner in my works; I merely threw one back. No offence taken, I hope. And now we have your full co-operation in the matter – as I'm sure we do – I will keep that video from the internet. Don't worry; you're the only one to have seen it, unless you've shown it to Mr Dark here. Ms Brice has it set to Private, so you and your canine paramour are quite safe from the public eye...so long as you abandon your opposition to my plans.'

Despite the nod Brice throws to Shah, the faintest hint of a blush can be seen rising beneath her foundation.

Those kids at the Spar. The messages from Chadwick's wife. Those gawpers on the bus. I'm guessing someone here has made a boo-boo with the Youtube settings.

'I'll have you arrested for blackmail. For drugging me like

that. For everything.' Chadwick's voice cracks. 'It may have escaped your notice that I'm a legally elected States Member...'

'You're a member alright,' yells Shah, his mood shifting violently as he gives Chadwick's table an angry thump. 'A big fucking *tool*, yes? You want me to ask this fellow here to arrest me?'

Officer Howe gives a tiny wave, mouths *hi*.

'You dog-fucking, car stealing, tool! And a coward, too, yes? You paid *him* to do it, didn't you!' yells Shah, pointing at me. 'You paid this scoundrel to kill Bill O'Malley for you!'

Somehow I've managed to take possession of the bottle of Macallan. Shah's accusation catches me mid-slug, and as I shake my head a thin stream of whiskey escapes from the neck, runs down my chin.

'For God's sake, Dark,' mutters Chadwick despairingly. Finding myself the sudden centre of attention I cough, spluttering like some fifteen year old with their first hoist of stolen Schnapps. Howe wrinkles his nose in disgust, whilst Bella Brice fixes me with the sort of stare Superman uses to melt girders in the films. How embarrassing.

'Henry Cavill,' I gasp, wiping down my whiskey-wet jaw with a sleeve. 'You missed that off your list. He's from Jersey too. Though in fairness Christopher Reeve was better.'

Which is true. That scene in the third one when Superman gets absolutely spangled in a mid-western bar? Genius. I remember watching the film with a feverish Louise when she was, what – two, three? – remember waking her from the doze she'd drifted into on our couch and pointing at the screen – *see sweetheart, even Superman gets drunk sometimes! See, it's okay!* –

only she wouldn't wake up because I'd overdone the Calpol and then her mother came downstairs and started screaming and stuff.

The bottle has found its way to my mouth again, its little glass beak poking past the flesh of my own, its malty innards spilling.

'Was that why you rolled Bill O'Malley off that cliff, Mr Dark?' Shah's voice is distant, muffled. 'To see if he could fly like your Mr Cavill?'

How floppy her little body had been. Who'd have thought Calpol could do that to you? She'd been fine, of course, that time, once her mother had got her to the hospital, but how floppy her body had been...

'You poor man.' Shah's voice adopts a softer, mocking tone. 'He threatened that cute little daughter of yours. The only thing in the world that makes your life worth living, and he threatened it. Of course with all that alcohol in your system you won't remember waiting for him outside his house – where they'll find your wallet – or the beating you gave him, or the moment you dragged him from the boot of a stolen Renault...'

No. Yes. No.

Something in me crumples. Nausea; physical, mental. I lose my balance, staggering forward into the table as my surroundings begin to dissolve. For a moment Shah, Brice and Howe merge into one giant, blurry hydra, their teeth bared, their long necks poised to strike. The Macallan makes a leap for my mouth again, though the Howe-head moves swiftly in to snatch the bottle from my hands.

'Congratulations by the way, Mr Dark.' My stomach

somersaults. I hear laughter from the Shah-head, the clap of soft, fleshy palms. 'You've just consumed close to six thousand pounds worth of whiskey!'

I gag, swallow, fist to mouth. My seared gullet bucks but somehow the whiskey stays down for now.

Deep breath. Focus. It'll pass.

Focus.

'The truth is, Mr Dark.' Shah moves in, his stale breath warm on my cheek. 'Mr O'Malley made a few bad decisions yesterday. He and the rest of those leeches at Terrata got greedy with my tower...'

'Mr Shah.' Brice's tone is firm. 'I'd advise you against...'

'My proxy buyer turned...*poxy*, shall we say,' he continues, his lips brushing the flesh of my ear. 'Poor Bill lost his nerve. Leapt out of the frying pan and into the sea.'

The table top turns to goo beneath my fingertips. My left knee gives once, again. Hot whiskey rises. The Macallan's staging a protest in my guts, smacking its placards furiously against my tonsils. *Out! Out! Out!*

'He refused to buy the tower for you so you had him killed.'

'Mr Chadwick, do shut up.'

'You'll go to jail for this!'

'I doubt that very much, Mr Chadwick.' Shah pulls away from me. 'With Bill out of the way and Terrata's major decisions being made by someone more...*amenable*...it's only a matter of time before that tower's mine. And oh, the plans I have for it!'

'Gurp,' I exclaim, drawing a frown from Bella Brice. It's okay though. I'm feeling better now. I've got this.

'To hell with it,' says Shah, fixing his electric cigarette with a disappointed look. 'Sometimes only the real thing will do.' Pocketing the silver tube he reaches down to the table and plucks out some chunky cigars from a metal box. He offers me one; I wave it away.

'Ah well. I shall celebrate myself,' he says, pulling a silver Zippo from his pocket.

'I don't see much to celebrate,' mutters Chadwick.

'You will, Mr Chadwick.' Flicking his Zippo Shah holds the flame to the end of his cigar. 'When Mr Dark returns the papers Mr O'Malley handed him yesterday at their little *meeting*, when you both walk away from this little saga, forever...tea and cakes all round, my friend. You'll have *plenty* to celebrate.' He lowers the tip of his cigar to the flame. 'The continued safety of Mr Dark's daughter, for starters.'

Louise. An invisible boot connects with the small of my back and I lunge forward, a thick rope of whiskey flying from my mouth and looping heavily over Shah's face and shoulders. The Arab cries out, the lit Zippo tumbling from his hand and down on to the tabletop, its little naked flame skidding the short distance before coming to rest against Gary Chadwick's left arm.

There's a moment of silence – a stunned Shah showered in belly-warmed whiskey, Brice's hands flying up to cover the shocked O of her mouth, Howe's eyes widening as they trace the Zippo's path – and then Chadwick goes up, the petrol in his clothes leaping to life in a sudden sheath of blue.

'Dark!' he shrieks, backing up into his seat as the flames engulf. 'Help me!' Wedged firm by the table edge he begins to thrash around as the flames leap up to his hair, hands and face, feeding gaily on the petrol in his pores. Howe makes a half-hearted lunge towards the blaze but a slap of flame beats him back; instead he turns to Shah – who's staring with fascinated horror at the human fireball before him – and starts screaming something about an extinguisher. Grimly conscious of the dousing I received back at the tower I can only back away, bumping into a fleeing Brice as the acrid smell of burning hair fills the galley, followed by the smell of something much, much worse.

Howe's found a fire extinguisher but it's too late for Chadwick, whose movements have become a hideous frenzy as he claws himself along the table edge in an attempt to break free from his flaming vice. The curtains behind him have caught now, as have his seat. The whole galley's about to go up.

The screams are pitiful. I try to help, universe, *truly I try to help*, stupidly reaching forwards but receiving only a lick of flame that snags my sleeve and flows like thin blue fluid up my arm. Oxidised atoms rub their hands in silent and spreading glee; the molecular knives and forks are out. I'm about to join Chadwick on the pyre.

No. I'm not going like this. My legs just won't let me – I'm shouldering past Howe now, already bidding my client a horrified farewell, racing up the steps as the cloth of my left sleeve surrenders in a flash of burning blue.

No. No. No.

My fingers grip the door frame. My shrieks merge with Chadwick's as I haul myself up the final step, up into the open air, the encircling sea. A sudden shock of pain as the flames reach my skin. The shocked O of an orange life ring on its clip, useless. It's raining out here, but not enough to matter, not enough to put me out.

I'm not going to make it – as I hurl myself over the rails I'm not going to make it and I'm burning, the flames have reached my hair, the agony is coming – and then the seawater hits me like a freezing wall and down I go into the darkness and the silence and the desperate bubbling panic of the sea.

18 – Old Chum

Daddy?

Clear as a bell, breaking through the treacle waffling of my watery cloak. A child's voice, soft and plaintive in the space between my ears.

Daddy?

A little boy in Spiderman face paint, cow-lick jutting from his forehead like an antenna. He's grinning up at the camera, one of those stupid full-teeth grins that kids throw at you when they just want you to put the thing away. Got a huge slice of birthday cake on the plate before him. Faintest hint of a kink in the side of his long head.

Daddy can I...?

The hair lengthens, the face paint reforming into a half-cocked attempt at Peppa Pig, the chin thinning, becoming more feminine, recognisable.

I release a bubbling depth-charge roar, tearing with splayed fingers at the image as it floats before me. Maybe it's a cry of sorrow, maybe it's a cry of relief; maybe it's just a simple and instinctive response to the nut-scrunching cold of the water. Either way it feels good to bellow like this, unheard and alone beneath the waves of the English Channel. Fitting, even.

For a moment I consider simply giving up and sinking to the sea bed, though the horrifying prospect of being forced to relive my life as it flashes before my eyes is enough to propel my limbs into motion. Wriggling free of my sweatshirt, scraping free my shoes I claw desperately up towards the green light of the surface. And somehow I make it, the air smacking my ears to life like some over-zealous midwife, filling them with a harsh treble hiss as spluttering and struggling I return to the muddled chaos of the world above.

I'm alive. My leap has taken me a few feet from *The Sabre*, and now I find myself staring up at its broad and unassailable starboard flank. Dark smoke billows from the cabin. An acrid, chemical stench fills the air, laced with something sweeter that I don't want to think about right now.

Having been herded on to the yacht at gunpoint Shah had cruised us a hundred metres or so out in to the bay, and as such both *The Sabre* and I remain a distance from the shore. The granite walls of the harbour are close enough to make out the iron rings set into their stone but there's no way I'll make it; not with these limbs, this body, in this state. I'll turn up eventually – stumbled upon by some lucky dog-walker – a shabby, fish-chewed thing caught on the edge of a rock pool perhaps, to be scooped up in a plastic bag, sealed with a knot and binned.

I wonder what the chances are of it being Chadwick's Labrador that finds me.

Chadwick. My client.

We set my client on fire.

Not yet. No time to process. If I'm to survive I need out of this water first and back up on to that burning boat. Orange flames swipe up at the roof from the galley windows like the paws of a playful cat; there's shouting within, clattering, the funnelled roar of a fire extinguisher being set off. Shah's fat head breaks above the side rail as he exits the cabin at the rear.

'Shah!' I call weakly, treading water with rapidly tiring legs.

A small wave breaks over my head. Muffle and bubbling. Salty cold. Air and then not air.

'Shah!' I call again, pointlessly, suddenly aware of a steadily rising buzz from the direction of the harbour where a speedboat is beginning to make its way towards us, its long green nose darting free past the granite walls, foam beginning to fly as it picks up pace.

The Sabre is moving now, too. The engine roars to life, propellers churning the water into an angry froth as the yacht swings its rear end round towards me. And there's Shah, his broad back hunched over the controls. Were I the pessimistic sort – which I am – I'd guess that he's planning to make mincemeat of me with *The Sabre*'s propeller.

I should probably be swimming away right now.

I can't.

Chopped white water flies. The propellers are metres away and closing. My world fills with a fury of foam and the scream of spinning metal.

What's that stuff they throw to sharks? Chum. I'm about to become chum. Wiggling my limbs like some spastic marionette I go nowhere. All is roaring and salt and cold and white. I slip under, my mouth filling, my brain already bidding a fond farewell to my fingers, hands and feet.

It's coming. You're *inventive*, Death – I'll give you that. It's coming.

And then, suddenly it isn't. The messy chug of the engine becomes a high-pitched drone as *The Sabre* begins to accelerate away, angling in towards the shallows of the bay. Dark smoke continues to billow from the cabin, and for a moment Shah is lost in its folds, hidden save for the glint of his grin and one raised middle finger, his left arm extended from the curtain of grey as the stricken yacht shrinks towards shore.

The gap left by *The Sabre*'s receding engine is filled by the whine of the approaching speedboat, at the wheel of which I spy a burly form in dark blue overalls. I raise an arm, registering with relief the wide, crew-cut head and dark brown overalls of Oscar de Gruchy, the Farmer's eldest son.

'Hold on Goldie!' The speedboat slows, tossing me in its wash. Oscar bends down, lifting and lobbing a meaty splat of rope out onto the water. With the remnants of my energy I kick over to it, clutching the thick length tightly as Oscar drags me in. Reaching down with a wide grin he hauls me up by the armpits and flops me roughly into the boat, where I lie shivering and stunned.

'N...N...Nick...'

'It's Oscar, Goldie. Heavy session?'

'...of time.'

'Oh.'

A shot rings out across the water. I fumble myself up with numbed, claw-like hands, peering over the side of the speedboat. The plume of smoke has thinned somewhat, and Shah's broad back can still be discerned at the controls as *The Sabre* hobbles shoreward. Somewhere far away a siren is wailing.

'Probably the engine firing, Goldie. You're a lucky man,' says Oscar, throwing a thick blanket over my shoulder. 'The old man was face down in the hall next to the phone when you called. Jed and me got there in time to hear everything that tosser was saying. Glad your knee survived.'

Lucky? Possibly. Calling up the Farmer whilst staring down the barrel of Howe's Glock in the car had been a desperate play, though it seems to have paid off. I'm not so sure Chadwick will be toasting his fortune any time soon though.

Oscar turns the boat round and we roar off back towards the harbour.

'D...d...dr...'

'Here,' says Oscar, pulling a fat-bottomed bottle from the recess of the boat. 'I'd say it's a medical emergency, wouldn't you?'

Cognac. Bless him. I fumble the cap with fingers of ice, gripping the curved base of the bottle with both hands and bearing the neck awkwardly to my lips. It isn't long before the Cognac's heat reaches my limbs and mind, settling like a smothering foam over the memory of Chadwick's screams, warming and dulling in equal measure.

Chadwick. We burned my client. I've a feeling they just shot him too.

I struggle up into a sitting position as Oscar leans hard on the throttle. *The Sabre*'s halfway to shore now. Howe's emerged from the cabin, his high visibility jacket clear against the lingering pall of smoke. He and Shah – small figures from here – are dragging a long black bundle between them, hauling it with bent backs towards the rear of the boat. I don't hear the splash it makes – we're too far away – but it makes me shudder all the same.

'Hang on in there,' yells Oscar as the speedboat accelerates, its sharp nose angling round towards the harbour's opening. Having cleared the granite walls we pass through a corridor of boats and softly bouncing buoys, eventually gliding in to our mooring against the harbour walls.

The Cognac's all but gone. With a final mouthful I raise a silent toast to poor Chadwick before rolling the bottle over the edge of the boat and into the black water, where it bobs and jerks before sinking without trace.

'Come on,' says Oscar, helping me up. 'I promised the old man I'd get you home safely. He wants a word.'

19 – The Bona Fide Bastard

Fathers, hey?

My own committed suicide when I was twelve years old. Jersey's town centre boasts several multi-storey car parks, and it was from the tallest of these that Lionel Francis Dark chose to launch himself one hot summer lunchtime, bidding farewell to this cruel hash of a world and putting a small group of unfortunately placed office workers firmly off their sandwiches in the process.

This was in the good old days before they installed anti-jump fencing, back when the pavement was your friend. Nowadays it's practically impossible to achieve such a grand and selfish exit. That fencing is tough, shrugging off pliers and hacksaws alike with a low metal giggle. A blow-torch would most likely do it, though let's face it; any suicide capable of that level of planning and dedication would probably already have been dead for weeks. No, car-park swan dives have been off St Helier's menu for a while.

Not so back then, however, on my father's Big Day. In my quieter moments I've often wonder whether he indulged in a backwards glance as he fell, whether he felt the sad gazes of my mother and I on his soon-to-be shattered form as he abandoned us to a future of which he no longer desired a part. Either way he'd hit the ground with a resoundingly final crump by the time we'd made it to the ninth floor parapet over which he'd vaulted, and had remained pretty much motionless from that moment on.

The look on my mother's face had been hard to describe; the silence between us awkward. She still had the car keys in her hand. We'd only come in to town for school shoes.

My mind has turned Daddywards because I could do with a little fatherly advice right now. Failing this, a few wise words from the Farmer – a man not dissimilar to my own in terms of relative age, temperament and mental instability – will do. I'm sure Oscar won't begrudge me a little of old Jean's verbal wool, steadily unwound, to help me navigate this maze. A little guidance is all I need. Something sensible and sage.

Oh well.

'Scum, Dark!' bellows Jean de Gruchy, fist raised, eyes slitted. 'Keepin' a woman chained to a wall like some sort of ruddy animal! Oh but she'll give them hell, my Abbie. She'll scratch 'em, kick their balls when they're not lookin'. Sideways, when their heads are turned. Like...like *this*. She was always good at that. Ball kicks. From the side. Oh Christ, Dark – just the thought of her eating woodlice off the floor and doin' her sit-ups in the dark – just the thought of her alone in that dungeon makes me want to start digging a ruddy tunnel. Can you find out where they're keeping her, Dark? Oscar will see that you're paid. He's a good boy, my Oscar. They're all good boys, you know, even Jed.'

Overcome with emotion the Farmer's grizzled face crumples like a flabby glove puppet being pulled into a fist. Tears stream from the corners of his eyes, tracing slick lines down to the savage tufts of his sideburns as his lower lip makes a leap for his nose.

I slap a hand on his shoulder, allowing what sympathy I have to bleed through the palm. Jean jerks his head up and down in stoic gratitude. *He knows, he knows.* 'Filthy degenerate bastards,' he croaks. 'My poor Abbie...but you're a good man, Dark. You'll get her back for me. I know you will.'

'Of course, Jean,' I lie, removing my palm with a final, filial slap.

Astonishing, what the human mind will do to keep its host afloat. The lies we tell ourselves, the webs we weave, those self-styled hammocks of filigreed untruth, unravelling even as they hold us trembling above the void.

'I know you will, Dark. I have faith in you,' gurgles Jean, breaking down completely.

Shuffling my filthy mug of Calvados to the kitchen window I peer out through the pane at the huddled chickens in the yard below. One of them has clambered on to an oil barrel, around the circumference of which it struts proudly, seemingly indifferent to the drizzle that has rolled its co-chickens into inanimate feathery balls. An old bicycle leans against a wall, rear wheel missing. Caught by the wind a torn tarpaulin flaps and falls over an untidy log stack like a blackened tongue in search of scraps. Beyond all this, past the leaning wooden fence, unkempt fields stretch off towards a distant nod of trees. In the middle of one of these the Farmer's youngest son Jed is operating a dirty yellow JCB earth mover, clawing a ragged trench in the ground with its thick metal scoop. Louie Jnr's car is buried out there somewhere, just off beyond those trees. Louie's car and so much else.

'I need a lift, Jean.'

'You need to rest, Dark,' says Jean, recovering his emotional poise via a short burst of facial stretches. 'Go get your head down for a bit.' His own quarter pint of Calvados sloshes round a battered tankard. 'Go on son,' he says, sipping it with a grimace. 'Get some rest.'

'I've slept.' Which is true. Having lost consciousness for a good half hour in the back of Oscar's Jeep I'd returned to the world jackhammer-skulled and groggy on the dirt road outside Jean's farm. Somehow Oscar had peeled me out of my swimming gear and into the old blue jumper and track suit bottoms that I've got on now. Babbling incoherently – I do that sometimes – I'd been borne through the farmyard on his shoulder, as though the young farmer were intent on feeding me headfirst to some hungry giant long grown bored of livestock baps. After a second dose of oblivion on the couch amidst the dusty clutter of the de Gruchy's lounge I'd awoken feeling grim, though a few shots of Calvados and eight Paracetamol have set me on a course of rightness on par with the tumbling rain outside.

'You look awful, my boy. Bloody awful,' frowns Jean, slamming back what's left in his tankard. Jean's not looking too hot himself; it's been a good few months since I've seen him, during which time his gut's gained a few inches on his belt and his shoulders – once wide and full in his tattered suit jacket – have begun a slow slide towards the floor. He wipes a hand across his upper lip, causing that bulbous nose of his to roll along the edge of his finger like a wayward tomato. 'Grab yourself another hour. At least until your clothes dry.'

I glance out the window again, spying my charred rags flapping mournfully on the washing line to which they've been pegged. They won't be dry anytime soon; although statistically possible that the raindrops will have fallen *around* them this past half hour it's hardly likely. As I watch my trousers come loose from their peg and blow off across the field towards the JCB, eventually snagging on its muddy wheel. The cabin's empty; through the deepening twilight I spot Jed trudging off across the field, absentmindedly wiping his hands on his dirty Man United football shirt as he goes.

'Can I use your phone, Jean?'

'I don't know, Dark. Can you?'

'I believe so.'

'Good for you, man. Bloody good for you.'

The Farmer turns ninety degrees to his left, his entire body moving at once, as though swivelling on some central bodylength stick. He lunges for the bottle of Calvados – last seen next to a bowl of rotting fruit on the kitchen table in the corner of the room – with one arm extended, fingers already clutching despite there being several steps to go. The trajectory is sound though something goes wrong mid journey and in a flash Jean has transformed himself into a four foot high pile of flesh, hair and wellington boots pressed snug against the kitchen door on the other side of the room.

'You okay, Jean?'

'Absolutely,' slurs the old man, hauling himself up with the help of the casing and leaving a fist sized smear of spittle against the cracked blue wood of the door. 'Must ask the boys to move that bloody table for me. Ridiculous having it so far away like that. Oh arse.'

Jean reaches out for his tankard, which, having slipped from his grasp at precisely the same moment that his metamorphosis commenced, now rolls slowly to a stop on the patch of stone floor from which he has just travelled. Closing one eye he stretches out his fingers as though willing the vessel to fly to him. I join my concentration to his, and for a moment it really does feel as though the tankard is about to leap through the air and into Jean's clutch. It twitches – it definitely twitches.

'You see that, son?'

'I saw.'

And then nothing. We fall silent, Jean leaning heavily against the door, the thick folds of his grizzled face kneading themselves into a hairy dough as he contemplates his next move.

'Chadwick's dead, Jean.'

'Chad *who*?'

'My daughter's in danger and I don't know what to do.'

Jean rolls his fat head towards me. 'Your *daughter*?' His forehead ruffles. 'Your *daughter*?' he repeats, seemingly confused.

And then Jean hurtles forwards, catapulted from the door – through which Oscar has just barged – like some grim and ragged boulder. He stagger-falls at speed yet somehow manages to grab the Calvados bottle on his way past the table, simultaneously pushing off its edge at an angle that propels him back towards his previous location. Having reached his tankard he deploys the ample air-bag of his arse, dropping to the floor with a huffed Jêrriais curse.

'Lovely,' he mumbles, grinning victorious from the floor and pouring himself a generous amount of Calvados before saluting Oscar with the bottle. 'How goes it, son of mine?'

'Feeling better Goldie?' asks Oscar, dismissing his father with a roll of the eyes.

Goldie. I do wish he wouldn't call me that. Makes me sound like a dog. A Labrador, even.

Chadwick. Oh god.

'Been better, Oscar. Been worse. Thanks again for the rescue.'

'Bastards,' gurgles the Farmer, attempting to retake his feet. 'Threatening a man and his knees like that...'

'You need help with anything?' Oscar raises his fists, adopting a boxing stance. With his blonde curly hair, blue eyes and chubby cheeks the twenty-five year old resembles a cherub on steroids, an angel not so much fallen as having taken a secondment from heaven to fight and play with cars. 'A little more midnight commando action?' he grins. 'We've still got the hats and face paint out in the shed. Last time was fun.'

Which it was, admittedly. I'd never seen a Scottish drug dealer spun round by his feet before. This situation is a little more delicate, however. Howe's complicity with Shah – and the implied compromising of our local force – has me rattled. My only hope is that Ledger has nothing to do with it. If Shah and his millions have got to *him* then I'm sunk. Again.

My only real hope is a solid *out*. These papers Shah mentioned, the ones supposedly handed to me by O'Malley, the same ones I must have passed over to Babs to get to Spickle; I need them back, whatever they are. Shah can have them in return for leaving me and Louise alone. With Chadwick gone the case is as good as over, anyway; I'll use the money he's already given me to hole up somewhere and drink this one out.

Might even throw back a few hundred pills this time and take a stab at not waking up again. Use the rest to invest in a blowtorch.

Shah first. Babs. Those papers.

'I need to use your phone, Oscar.'

'What's with this bloody phone fixation, Dark?' grumbles the Farmer, generously anointing the kitchen floor with Calvados as he attempts to retake his feet.

'Sure. The landline's at the end of the hallway there.'

I nod my thanks, fighting the urge to reach over and hug him – wrap myself round that big right leg of his – and embarrass us all. Kindness does this to me sometimes. Guess I'm a softy at heart.

Tears welling I leave Oscar hoisting his father into a chair. The day's events are beginning to catch up with me, and it is on weak legs and with an aching, hazy head that I slide down the hallway wall in the direction of the telephone.

Still, things could be worse. My burns from *The Sabre* blaze are minimal, confined mostly to a patch of blisters on the back of my left hand, and Jean's Calvados is the best I've tasted in years. *Always pays to look for the silver lining*, as Dr Griffiths used to tell me. *There's one around every cloud.*

I wonder what Gary Chadwick would say to that.

Those screams.

The smell of searing flesh.

Focus, Dark. Focus.

The telephone is wall-mounted, a squat brown thing with an old school circular dial mechanism. Inserting my finger into the 6 I revolve and release, drawing an odd satisfaction from the sound of the dial as it clicks back down to zero. 4 next. Then 1.

Then what? I'm used to dialling Babs up on mobile; my finger-muscle memory isn't keyed up for this rotary business. I close my eyes and try dialling up his number on an imaginary mobile. I've only just recalled the first three digits when the hypothetical handset bursts into flames and now I'm poking my finger into the hot slush of Gary Chadwick's eye and there's screaming and the stench of burning skin and suddenly I'm back in the hall again, gasping and sobbing and scared...

'You alright down there?' calls Oscar.

'All good,' I manage. 'All good.'

Perhaps I should take the Farmer's advice and lie down somewhere. Things seem to be coming apart. Despite the evening's cool I'm sweating profusely. The telephone trembles wildly in my hands.

Attempting to banish thoughts of poor Chadwick from my mind I focus on a mounted photograph of Jean and Abigail, he grinning goofily in a blue tux like Charles Darwin on a first date, she in a tight fitting black number that looks about as comfortable as the smile she's got stapled to her face.

The flames and screaming recede. My fingers find their way.

Rasp, whirr, click. Rasp, whirr, click.

Babs answers on the fourth ring, his familiarly plum tone causing yet another swell of emotion and forcing me to gargle back tears.

'Marigold! About bloody time! Been trying to get hold of you.'

'Not having the best of days, Babs.'

'I'll bet. How was the head this morning?'

'Better than it is now, Babs. Listen. Those papers I gave you...'

'Remember them, do you?'

'Not exactly.'

'Not surprised. Commendable display of shitfacery last night, old chap. Really put the effort in there. Off your bloody head you were. Making no sense at all. All dogs and Martello Towers.'

'The papers, Babs.' I lay my slick forehead against the cooling plaster of the wall. Lovely simple things, walls. Straight up, no messing. 'The ones O'Malley gave me. Where are they?'

'Right. Those. Well, I sent them off to Spickle like you asked, though that's a bloody tale in itself, what with having to get young Jenny at the Seymour to scan them in on her printer thing so I could email them over, me being a total bastard Luddite when it comes to these things, as you know...'

'The papers, Babs.' The hallway wall bounces twice off my forehead, or maybe it's the other way round.

'Jolly ho. To the point. Those papers. Some sort of garbled family lineage, as you and I suspected – all those names and dates and what have you – Corbet this and bloody Corbet that right up until the fifties where, as you yourself pointed out last night before buggering off to make an arse of yourself with that barmaid...

'The *fifties*?'

'Yes, the fifties. Where it kind of ends. Sort of.'

'Sort of what?'

'Sort of the family tree ends, but then there are all these other documents as well...copies of certificates, property transfers, newspaper clippings and so on. It's all there, like O'Malley promised. And you'll never guess... '

'Promised who?'

'What? Oh. *You*, you daft twot! Christ Dark, don't tell me it's all a *total* blank?'

'Yes. No. Sort of. Please, Babs...go on.'

'Well, as O'Malley explained to you in Chambers...'

'Chambers.' Of course. My flashback from earlier coheres, forming itself into something akin to a memory. Chambers, with its long, dark bar and shadowed booths; that's where I met O'Malley yesterday afternoon after our lunchtime scuffle, tucked away at a table in the back. I remember now.

'Yes, Dark. There. According to you O'Malley asked you to track Moses Corbet's last remaining relative down. Said he couldn't be seen to be doing it or else he'd get his fat Irish botty spanked by some nasties on his tail. Offered to pay you for your services. I'm guessing that's one you're going to have to write off. You've heard the news, yes? The Irish Sausage Smuggling Society are a man down.'

'Yes.' For a moment I'm crushed to the hallway wall by the enormity of it all. O'Malley, Chadwick, my visible and undeniable involvement with both. Don't think I've been in this much shit since that incident with the port-a-loo on my thirty-fifth birthday.

'So did Spickle find him?'

'The bastard? Yes!'

'*Bastard*? Why? What's Spickle done now?'

'Not *Spickle,* old chap. A bastard. An actual *bona fide* bastard. Spickle found him!'

'Babs. Please.' I knead the centre of my forehead, trying to pinch away the ache within. 'Imagine you're talking to a six year old child. A really stupid one. A retard, if you will.'

'Jolly ho. So listen. Moses Corbet had a son and a daughter in wedlock, yes? Though after that the whole descendant thing goes a bit blank, just a bloody great wall of no-one. Except according to those papers O'Malley gave you Corbet went and had a son off radar. When Mrs Corbet wasn't looking, if you get my drift. Old bugger kept it all hush hush but got the guilts enough to leave a few bits for the poor bastard – literally, ha! – in his will. Clever old Mr Spickle was able to trace the bloodline through to the present day on that computer of his. Turns out there's only the one descendant left – Kyril Higgins, or Higley, or something like that. Lives up near Manchester. Well, *lived*. In a home, poor chap. Doo-lally. Paranoid schizophrenia, amongst other things.'

'*Lived*, Babs? Where is he now?'

'*Kaput*, old chap. Found swinging in his room not two weeks ago. All rather suspicious, apparently.'

The phone drops from my ear. So that's what this is all about. The discovery of a legal heir to Corbet's estate would have presented a serious challenge to Terrata's – and through them Shah's – purchase of the tower. With no other way of blocking the deal flagging up Corbet's hidden bloodline was O'Malley's last play. Having got into bed with the Devil it appears that the Irishman had been quietly trying to shuffle out unnoticed, and in doing so had got himself shuffled over the edge of a cliff.

'Dark? You there?'

'Yes, just...Babs...did Shah know anything about Higgins?'

'Oh bloody hell yes. Spickle's done a grand job of digging up some emails between Shah and his fund manager, a woman called...'

'Bella Brice.'

'Bloody well done, Dark. Glad to hear your brain hasn't entirely fallen out of your arse. Anyway, yes – turns out our Arab friend found out about Higgins a few weeks back. And then Higgins died. Um.'

'You've got those papers in front of you, Babs?'

'Well, almost.' The sound of rustling, a light thump. 'Hang on. Now I do. Right here. Why?'

'I need them back. Urgently. I need you to get them to me.'

Silence on the line.

'Babs? You still there?'

'BUGGERATION!' The Farmer's voice roars down the hall from the kitchen, followed by the smash of breaking glass. Oscar can be heard swearing loudly; through the gap in the door I can see a tatty slice of Jean's torso, horizontal again and spread across the floor.

'Babs?'

'Still here, old chap. Listen.' An edge of concern creeps into Babs' voice. 'Dead developers. Arab millionaires. This is all getting a bit...you know. *Serious.*'

'Stick with me, Babs. I'll explain. I need those papers.'

'The Ambassadeur again?'

'Not a good idea. St Helier. The Lamplighter. One hour.'

'I'll do my best, Dark. Buses etcetera. Would drive but am somewhat sozzled at the moment.'

'They took your license off you, Babs. Twice.'
'True.'
'And you don't have a car.'
'That too.'
'The Lamplighter. One hour.'
'Jolly ho.'

20 – A Little Bit Flat

Louise's mother had insisted on the move. This was before the injunction, before the incident with Buttons and the lawnmower (to this day I swear it was *her* that left the hutch unlocked), back when – at least to my eyes – we stood a chance of working things out. The marriage was over, yes, but that didn't mean we needed to lose the house. We could do this like adults. Cohabit. I'd been perfectly willing to funnel myself, a mattress and a few essential possessions into the spare room downstairs, promising (on my knees, repeatedly) to keep to my side of the building, to come and go via the plastic side door exiting onto the lane that ran parallel to our garden – I'd promised all of this, sensibly, reasonably...and then unreasonably, louder, wetly, mouth squished to the metal interior of the police van as they wrestled me away the third, fourth and fifth times, promised that if she only gave it another go I'd quit the drinking, kick the habit, plug the stopper, get counselling, get help, see another doctor – a different, *better* doctor – attend anger management classes, get hypnosis, change my pills, remember to take my pills, stop taking my pills, have a lawyer draw up terms, *her* terms, her way, I'd sign it, I'd sign anything if she gave me one more chance and let me move back into the back room once the fire damage got fixed died down or the door got re-hinged or they replaced the ceiling where I'd hacked hysterically up through the lounge floor with a hammer, I'd sign anything if they'd just let me out of this van and undid these cuffs these bloody cuffs ow those cuffs you bastards you pig scum filthy Nazi bastards those cuffs those ow those cuffs my wine –

'You sure you'll be okay, Goldie?'

I look up from my wrist, suddenly conscious that I've been massaging it for the past half minute or so. Night has fallen. We're cruising along the Avenue – the island's only dual carriageway – on the southern coastal approach to town, bearing down on the residential block that houses my ex-wife's flat. Perhaps it's the proximity to her abode that has me on edge, or perhaps it's something about the expansive interior of Oscar's jeep and its heavy rumbling wheels that brings back memories of the various police vans whose guts I've graced. Either way my nerves are shredded like a bunny in a mower (again; not my fault).

'I drink to forget, Oscar. Did you know that?'

Oscar nods uncomfortably.

'I drink to forget because sometimes...sometimes I get sloppy and forget to drink. And that's a dangerous thing to do, Oscar. Because that's when it all comes back. The insanity of all this.' I wave the Calvados bottle out at the temporary arrangement of brick and flesh and lights before us. 'Little beetles rolling dung balls up a hill, Oscar, that's all we are – little beetles pushing dung up a hill to see who can stack the biggest pile. That was me for *years*, Oscar. That's all I was. Just this little clicky *thing* rolling shit up a hill.'

But Oscar merely shrugs.

'And I wanted to be more,' I continue, eyes welling, surprised at this sudden spill of words. 'For Louise. For my daughter. I wanted to be so much more. Something better. An example, Oscar. An *example*. But I forgot about the black hole in my head, see? It's an illness, you know. Not a lifestyle choice, like her mother used to claim; it's a fucking *illness*. And we went swimming this time and it sucked us all in. And I know I'm not making sense, because they threatened my daughter, Oscar...they threatened Louise, and she's all...she's all...'

My throat tightens. I've no idea why I'm saying what I'm saying. Lowering my head I allow the wet warmth of my eyes to empty down my cheeks, shoulders bucking as a high pitched whining squeezes from the back of my throat. I weep softly for several seconds as Oscar fiddles awkwardly with the radio. They're playing that song by Phil Collins, the one with the drums from that advert with the monkey suit. I've always hated Phil Collins. And we went to the zoo once, me and Louise, went to see the orangutans...

'You okay, Goldie?'

I wish he wouldn't call me that.

'Yes,' I wheeze, taking a long, throat-searing pull of Calvados. 'Yes I'll be fine.'

Making use of a red light I excuse myself at the Esplanade, opposite the HSBC building. Having given the young farmer a salute I slam the door of the Jeep and stagger up on to the pavement, watching on unsteady legs as it pulls off to merge with the glimmering string of east-bound traffic. Pausing for a moment to gather myself I fill my lungs with the chill November air, feel its clarifying pinch upon my skin. No more talk of black holes and beetles; there are things out here in the real world that are within my power to fix, and fix them I shall.

The night sky is starless, the pavement, road and buildings washed a sickly sodium yellow. Across the dual carriageway – way off where the sea used to be before they built all over it – Cineworld's broken sign flickers: INTERSTELLA. Past this the horizon attempts to assert itself again, only to be shoved to the deck by the lean glass flank of Fitness First and then elbow-dropped into submission by the Belsen-esque slab of the Radisson Blu hotel.

Having gathered my mind and soul into the mental equivalent of a plastic bag I stumble off down the pavement, dodging the cracks so that I won't go to Hell. Past the lit fronts of the banks I stagger, past the finance houses, their dung-rollers (enough!) long since blown by money-whetted appetites into the cocktail bars and high-end eateries that pepper the town. High on its rocky bluff the white dome of Fort Regent glints in its own light like the hairless pate of some sick old clown, the grinning rictus of its lower face long since blown into an ugly avalanche of architectural gore.

I turn in off the Esplanade, moving under a curved stone archway and down a side street formed by the back end of a multi-story car park not dissimilar to the one from which my father flung his soon-to-be corpse. Adjacent to this stands a tall, sandstone-coloured building – one of Terrata's finest hives of 'luxury' flats – a gleaming block of cunning modernity with interiors so small they may as well have been cored from a concrete megalith with the tip of a potato peeler. Louise's mother scurried into this one a few years back, taking my daughter with her – no doubt waving with forced smiles at their own reflections in the spotless lift as it bore them up to the security of the sixth floor. Even now it makes me smile to imagine my ex-wife nervously peering over the balcony, gazing down the length of the building and wondering whether Bad Daddy Kong could reach them up here.

It shouldn't make me smile, but it does. Makes me want to cry as well, though I've no tears left just now. I'm all cried out.

The glass door to the ground level reception area is locked and rattles heavily in its frame when I give it what for. I easily pick out my ex-wife's buzzer on the panel – it's the only one without a name on it, just a white strip of cardboard behind the little rectangle of plastic.

As if that's going to put me off trying. As if by pretending she isn't here I'll forget all about her.

Though perhaps I should. Perhaps I should just hurry on towards the Lamplighter, where Babs will already be waiting for me, a beer on the bar.

Do you see this, ye cruel and judging gods? Can you see me, oh scornful universe? Beer on the bar, my *beer's already on the bar* yet here I am – and here I feel a sudden and confirming surge of pride – here I am resisting, defending, *protecting* what's left of my family.

Shah's a dangerous man – ask Bill O'Malley, ask Gary Chadwick – so I'm leaving nothing to chance. I'm here for Louise, for her mother, to warn them, to get them out and to safety, at least until this whole sick game plays out. Until the mad Arab gets his papers back. Until everything's returned to the way it was before I got involved in this mess. Until the threat to my daughter is gone.

Still no response from the sixth floor. I let the final buzz ring for over a minute, leaning heavily against the door, hot breath misting the glass.

Nothing. I contemplate smashing my way in – there's a large rock over there that would probably do the trick – and taking the lift up to see them. Of course Louise's mother's door will no doubt be locked as well, and smashing my way through *that* might take some doing. Might give a slightly muddled message as well. Maybe not.

Instead I write DANGER! in the condensation left by my breath, only backwards so Louise's mother will read it the right way round when she next exits the lift. Which all is good, except halfway through I realise that although I'm doing the letters backwards they're in the wrong order, so that all Louise's mother will read is !REGNAD, which is bad. I try again, right to left this time, on a new piece of glass, with new breath. The N is the hardest. Can't quite work it out. After my third try I get angry and give up, urinating loudly against the door in protest.

Bladder emptied, inside left trouser leg soaked due to an unexpectedly heavy after-flow, I head back out on to the Esplanade, up past the banks and the Finance houses towards the pubs and the clubs and the dungy hub of things. Time to get O'Malley's papers back to Shah and put and end to this. And if Babs has done the decent thing and made sure that beer of mine is already on the bar, then so much the better. I think I've earned it, don't you?

21 – Bits and Babs

Plump. Rosy. Ruddy of jowl. They don't make milkmaids like this one any more. She squats on a stool, shoulders bowed, happy face flattened in profile against the cow's tawny flank. Her fingers are meshed adroitly with its flesh; at her feet sits a metal pail into which the faintest splashes of white can be seen tumbling from the animal's udder. Beyond woman and beast the horizon is a grin of blue and green. Birds freckle the cloudless sky. The sun is high.

She's thinking of her husband, the hopeless drunk. He's off on a bender right now, having left her alone with the cows for the whole weekend. She's thinking that if only she could communicate this fact to the soldier stood next to her – a tall fellow, trim moustache, hair neatly combed – then maybe they could strike something up, maybe she could gain an ally to help her out of the mess she's in. It's her own fault; her mother had warned her about that man of hers, said he was a wrong 'un from the start.

For now though the milkmaid is staying coy. Affecting distraction so as not to scare the soldier off. Just keeps rolling that soft pink flesh between her fingers, her smile fixed.

Alas, she has it all wrong. Sullen in his starched red and white, cocked cap set high upon his broad head, the soldier doesn't give a musket ball for the glimpsed cliff of the milkmaid's breasts, nor the pretty face of the dark-eyed Jersey whose udder she is emptying. His mood is dark (someone's filmed him having sex with a dog) and the gun by his side is oiled and loaded, ready to silence both cow and maid if a stray drop of spattered milk should trouble the shine on his shoes.

There'll be hell, though, should that musket be raised. The rugby player to his left – an absolute bull of a man with a Judge Dredd jaw – has only to reach across with his...

'Come on man, make your fucking mind up! We're gasping!' yells a red-faced chap on the other side of the bar. I return to my senses, snapping back to the task at hand.

'So what'll it be then, old chap?' Babs raises an eyebrow.

What pretty shields these beer pumps bear. On every one a story, to each a tale.

'Pint of Bombardier,' I say, with a nod at the soldier. 'Thanks.'

I've made it to the Lamplighter. It's noisy in here, noisy and cramped, the tiny pub squeezed tight with a mixed crew of piss-heads and soon-to-be-pissed-heads. The live football ended a few hours ago and Saturday night is off and running.

'Coming up,' says the barmaid, gripping the pump.

'Bloody good choice,' pipes Babs from the high stool next to mine. 'Lovely kick to it, that stuff. Hint of musket. Slight cannonbally aftertaste. Maid's Pail for me though, thanks. Cheers.'

'Cheers.' We clink glasses, before hurling our pints back in one. Babs doesn't even swallow.

'So then,' he says.

'So then.' Gas ripples up my pipes, caught deftly in the curl of my fist. If I were a magician there'd be a colourful handkerchief stuffed in there, some other surprise designed to bring joy and amaze. As it is there's just stale air that flutters free when I flex my hand like some invisible and slightly smelly dove.

'Been quite a day, Babs. Haven't had a day like this since this last time it was quite a day.'

'Which was?'

'Quite a day.'

Man down. Two of them. Babs and I raise our empty pint glasses in unison, silently holding them aloft until the barmaid's finished serving old Red Face over there his lager. Snatching our empties with a shake of the head she sets about refilling with a look of open disgust.

Around us the Lamplighter is bustling with beery noise, the air thick with the smell of damp clothes, mild to moderate body odour and overflowing drip trays. Up on the wall-mounted TV screens a lager advert gives way to the muted opening sequence of the local news. No-one cares. Over on the corner couch some spotty chap's strumming a badly tuned guitar, singing something about *meeting girls* and *factory walls*. A sizeable lady to my right asks if they sell nuts. Someone somewhere shrieks like a horse.

'Well you will insist on inserting yourself into these...*situations*, old boy,' says Babs, once we've been reloaded.

'Man's got to pay the bills.'

'Yes but there are jobs and there are *jobs*, Dark. I seem to recall you getting into less trouble when you sat behind a desk.'

'No more desks, Babs. Last one nearly killed me.'

'Stack some shelves then. Push some trolleys. Clean a road. Or better still, sign on like the rest of us. With your condition there must be something you could claim. Insanity, for starters.'

'I'm still useful. I still have a use.'

'One wonders whether poor old Gary Chadwick would agree.' Babs leans into his new pint, white moustache settling softly over the rim like a shaggy dog dropping on to its favourite rug. 'He'll turn up, you know, Dark. They always do. Sea's got a way of confessing itself. And then what?'

'No idea,' I shrug, seeking guidance in the froth of my ale. 'I honestly don't know.'

'You're a wanted bloody man, Dark,' Babs goes on. 'If what you've told me is true – about your crazy Arab and his plans – they'll probably try and pin this second death on you as well. You need an escape route, old chap! I'd be on the first boat to St Malo if I were you.'

It's certainly an option. I've a fake passport at home which would do the job should Ledger have put Customs on alert. But where would I run to? And what about Louise?

'I'm not running, Babs. I've done nothing wrong.'

'Whatever. Point is, old boy,' says Babs, pausing to belch into his sleeve, 'this has got to end somewhere. You're up against mega-money here. Shah's got friends in elevated positions. The island's been wiggling its arse in the UAE's face for years now...'

'...and Shah's a sniffer.'

'Sniffer? Ha! The bugger's climbed right in and made himself a home, Dark! Got squidillions in trust over here. Investment funds, property holdings, you name it. Pretty much a poster boy for the local pinstripe brigade. Look.'

Babs reaches along the bar for a discarded copy of the Evening Post. Folding the right page into place he gives the headline a knowing tap: ARAB DELEGATION TO

STRENGTHEN TIES WITH FINANCE. The text keeps drifting but with one eye closed I'm able to pin it down long enough to spot the reference to our man.

...Treasury Minister's visit to Dubai last month in a bid to consolidate business links with the Middle East. Visitors to this week's Jersey Finance conference have included Prince Saif Al Jabar and businessman Hassan Shah, the latter of whom recently caused controversy in Cornwall with his purchase of medieval fort Pednevil Keep. Dubai-born Shah's plans to convert the fort into a corporate event suite were met by fury from...

'Makes you wonder why they don't just give him Corbet's tower and have done with it.'

'Ha! And risk the peasants' fury?' scoffs Babs. 'There'd be a bloody riot. Apparently that Cornwall thing got nasty enough. No, we all *know* that foreign money has the run of this place...but it's quite another thing altogether to openly replace the Jersey flag with a set of splayed arse-cheeks and a dollar sign.' Babs flings back the rest of his pint. 'Of course there are *other* ways of doing these things, as I suspect your man O'Malley could have told you. Like I said, Shah has friends in high places. Whereas you, old chap...have no-one.'

That's not quite true. I've got Ledger, I think, though Howe's complicity still troubles me. If he and Super Mario are chums then I'm sunk. No way of knowing without turning myself in.

'You're dealing with an old boys' network here, Dark,' Babs continues. 'Decades of palm-greasing and back-scratching and lord knows what else. And if Shah really wants that tower – which you tell me he does – then you can bet some of our high-ranking pinstripe army will be prepared to move Heaven and earth to keep him happy. Can't have all that Arab money going elsewhere, can we?'

'I wonder what made O'Malley change his mind?' I ponder out loud. 'About selling the tower on to Shah. Why sabotage the deal?'

'Who knows? Stroke of conscience, perhaps. Or maybe he just didn't relish the prospect of climbing into bed with a homicidal maniac. Lord knows my wife never did. Two more, please love.' Babs flicks the barmaid an obscene wink. 'Be easier if we just swapped sides hey? But don't worry, you're doing well, you're doing well. Now listen, Dark,' he says, growing suddenly grave and tapping the wedge of folded papers resting between us on the bar. 'Here's the question. What are you going to do with these?'

O'Malley's dog-eared pile, he means. Attached now to the sheaf of pages by a single paper clip is the sheet of A4 upon which Spickle has provided the dead heir Higgins' details; phone numbers, addresses and an annotated Google Map of Salford. Hacked emails too, including correspondence from Bella Brice to a foreign party – clearly team Shah – detailing the discovery of a Manchester-based fly in his ointment.

'*Mr Higgins refuses to acknowledge your offer,*' Babs reads slowly, eyes twinkling. '*Further instructions urgently required.* It's all bloody there, Dark. Enough to raise some serious eyebrows.'

'I can raise eyebrows just by taking off my trousers, Babs. It's evidence that's important. Illegally hacked emails tend to get cut down in court. Plus there's Spickle to consider. I wouldn't want to drag him into this.'

'You couldn't drag John Spickle anywhere. Have you seen the size of him these days? And who said anything about using them as evidence? Just wave them under the right noses, set loose the dogs of law. Jolly ho!'

Fresh pints ahoy. We sip, swallow, sigh.

'To poor old Kyril Higgins,' says Babs.

To Bill O'Malley. To Gary Chadwick. To me.

'To Kyril Higgins.' We clink glasses.

'Bet the bugger didn't know what hit him. Doesn't pay to be bonkers, you know,' sniffs Bab. 'Especially when you've got a billionaire Arab trying to stuff your straightjacket full of money.'

'Do they still use straightjackets, Babs?'

'No idea. I'm sure we'll find out one day.'

'Indeed.' Babs throws his head back with such gusto that for a moment it looks like he's going to tear himself off at the cheek. Having hurled the rest of his pint into his beerhole he lowers his glass on to the bar next to mine so that their sides are touching. A tender move; a hug, of sorts.

I belch, quietly. Three ales down. I've been here precisely sixteen minutes. Like visitors at an art gallery Babs and I sink rapidly into silent contemplation of the empty glasses before us. Foam smears the sides of each like empty speech marks. Tiny bubbles slide and burst.

'We're not doing too well, are we Dark,' muses Babs softly.

'No,' I say. 'We are not.'

'Felicity would not be best pleased.'

'Felicity would give us The Look.'

'I remember it well, old chap.'

'Give me grace to accept with serenity the things I cannot change...'

'I dreamt about her last night. Felicity. We were sat in our circle again and you were crying, as usual. That high pitched back of the throat thing you always used to do. Really used to irritate me, that. Sorry, but it did.'

'...courage to change the things which should be changed...'

'E.T. was there, in this dream. That little alien thing with the big eyes and long neck from the film. Like a child-sized turd on legs. You know the one. He was there as well, listening to you crying, no doubt getting rather irritated by it too. And then all of a sudden he *was* Felicity – bit bloody weird it was, I'd been eating brie – he was Felicity and he lifted that long middle finger of his, like this...and it started glowing, and he slowly moved it towards your forehead.'

'...and the wisdom to distinguish the one from the other.'

'And you just reached up and bit it off. Just like that. Snap. Bit the whole bloody thing off and spat it back into his big alien face. I woke up screaming to find myself in the middle of pissing the bed. Except I wasn't on the bed, I was on the floor, so I pissed all over that instead. Not a great start to the day.'

Courage to change the things which should be changed. The words return to me as something on the TV screen catches what's left of my attention. We're still in the middle of the local news, only now the camera's pulling a slow-panned shot of a drizzly St Aubin's harbour, against the moorings of which can be seen a familiar and smoke-damaged yacht.

'Had worse, mind. That time I tried to end it all in the

Peugeot with the hose and exhaust pipe and all that. Forgot I had the bloody air-con on. Whole day I was slumped there, until the neighbours pulled me out. Middle of summer it was. Underpants only. My thighs were practically soldered to the leather....'

Babs babbles on. My eyes are glued to the TV screen, where the camera has got up close to the *Sabre*. We're treated to a brief tour of the fire blackened cabin, shots of singed sails and melted tarp. Some shaky mobile footage also – taken by someone at the harbour – of the stricken vessel heading back in to shore.

'Courage,' I mutter, only vaguely conscious that I am doing so.

'Then there was that time I went into work dressed as Batman. Did I ever tell you about that, Dark? Right in the thick of it I was. Lowest ebb. Ended brownly, that one. All-in-one body suits, bad idea. The lunge for my ex-secretary's letter opener got horribly misconstrued. Was facing an attempted murder charge for a while....'

The TV screen fills with the image of Hassan Shah, sky blue sweater draped over his shoulders and looped in a tidy knot beneath his throat, dark hair slicked flawlessly back from his creaseless brow. Black shades hide black eyes, a blacker soul. *Hassan Shah,* reads the caption at the bottom of the screen. *Investor.*

Murderer, it should read. *Invader.*

'...face down in a urinal...'

Is it my imagination or did Shah just lower his sunglasses and wink at me? Am I seeing things or is he actively seeking me through the lens, goading me to action with that half-formed sneer? His lips move soundlessly but I can read them, I can make out the word as it forms: *surrender*.

Things which should be changed.

Invader.

Come to burn us down.

And suddenly I see it whole. I know what I must do.

There are no French muskets this time, no boatloads of soldiers, no blazing brands bearing down upon the streets and houses of St Helier. No Nazis either, save those two goons from earlier. There's just money. Just one more madman with too much money, come to hack off his slice of our coastline, come to carve his slice of rock. And who is there to stop him?

Yes, I know now what I must do. For Louise, my darling daughter, for *all* the children of this tiny blessed isle of ours, for the countless generations of Jerseymen to come, for poor old Gary Chadwick, whose charred, bullet-holed corpse must even now be drifting around the coastline he swore to protect, for Alice Chadwick, for little Kevin, for Bill O'Malley and Salma Hayek and Peter Falk and that woman in Mothercare and the universe and for me, for *me*, Marigold Dark, Saviour of the Islands, Defender of the Channel...*I know what I must do.*

We will not surrender. *I* will not surrender.

'Can't help but notice that you're blubbing again, old chap,' says Babs. 'Won't do at all. Same again?'

'Same again.'

'Jolly ho.'

22 – Off to Work We Go

and the pavement says hi and where is he let me up and back in at the red faced shit ok Babs no I'm ok it's just blood give me those I know what I'm going to no I'm alright Babs honestly neon lights oh neon lights *she went under you know when you weren't watching* I know what I must do to protect *you were drunk* and who'd have thought it was this far I should bounce on a few cars whilst I'm here like Super Mario boink boink boink it's buried Iain and there's very little

cross town traffic

who's that on the desk if not my adopted mother how's it going Jan what's Mr Moustache like in bed and have you seen these by the way Higgins Higgins look Higgins Chadwick is oh Chadwick is sshhhhh shhhh musn't say *Chadwick is underwater like* you will? No these aren't tears just a cold yes. You will? Tell him Detective Dark sends his love and one more thing, just one more thing yes taxi please yes thanks Jan you've always been my favourite yes to St Ouen! St Ouen! Because I'm sleeping there, you dig? Because I know what I must do zzzzzz

zzzzzzzz ok man ok man it's only piss yes this is it she paid you my mother paid your fare at the station no need to be so bloody rough oh bye then bye bye leave me ha ha I'm an expert in this field now come on Jed have left the keys have left the keys oh you big monster *she's never coming back* and how does this thing wooooaaaahhhh boy woooooahh boy and here we come you grinning fat-jowled *shit* here I come and one more thing Mr Shah, just one more thing, just one more thing....

hi ho, hi ho

I know what I must do

brmmm brmmm brmmm

23 – The Earth Moves

It's yellow. Don't ask me why. She just wants it to be yellow. Not pink, like the other little girls at nursery, not red like the one we saw in the toy shop, but yellow. *Wan' wellow pwam. Wan wellow one.* Wants a little yellow suited dolly to go in it as well, so her mother has dragged out an old custard coloured sleeper from the leftover baby clothes and slipped it over the tiny plastic human we've bought her to push around. It's an expensive one with moving eyelids and soft blond hair and a button to make it talk and everything. *Mummy I'm thirsty. Mummy I need a poo.*

We've wrapped them – baby entombed in pram – and left them at the foot of the bed for her to find when she bounces in, which she's bound to do any moment now. I know this because I'm awake, which can only mean that something woke me, which means that tiny feet have quit their bed and are padding eagerly across the landing, or will be any moment now.

Her mother is asleep behind me, or at least pretending to be. I can feel the warm pressure of her against my backside, most probably the press of her own. We've slept like this – back to back, buttocks to buttocks – for as long as I can remember. Things aren't great between us these days and haven't been for a long time though still the contact's nice, a reminder that on some basic level we're still in this together. The three of us; my wife, my daughter and I.

A real mattress-hogger, my wife. Forever trying to push me out. She's been at it again last night, for I find myself teetering on the edge of the bed, the muscles of my right arm and side instinctively tensed in an attempt to arrest the fall. As the grogginess begins to lift I become gradually aware of my upper body surrendering to the slow tug of gravity. It's probably time to do something about it, though perhaps if I can just hold on a little longer I can time my tumble with Louise's entrance, start her birthday with a laugh. She loves it when I do things like that. Loves it when her Daddy clowns around.

The air feels unusually cold against my cheek, the draft so strong that I can feel it ruffling my hair. Has someone left a window open? Did I forget to shut the front door again?

A cry.

Daddy can I...?

Louise, is that you? Sweetheart? My tongue tears free from the roof of my mouth with an audible rasp as I try to call her name.

That cry again. Multiple cries, all around me. They don't sound human though, and they certainly don't sound like my daughter. More like the squawking of birds.

Seagulls.

I can hear seagulls.

Slipping now from the side of the mattress I extend my palms, expecting to encounter the carpet of the bedroom floor, gasping in surprise as I collide instead with something cool and flat. It judders upon impact, a dull sound like struck plastic.

I try to force open my eyes, gasping in pain as the hard light blades my brain. Too bright; it's too bright to be indoors.

But then this isn't my bedroom, is it?

We're not back then at all, are we?

No. So where the hell am I?

The remaining tatters of my dream are wrenched from me by a gust of wet, salty air. Something sharp is gnawing at my shoulder. I reach up with my right hand, exploring the wide fabric strip stretched tight across my chest. Feels like a seatbelt, which would suggest that I'm in some kind of vehicle.

A low moan escapes me.

My eyes are beginning to adjust to the hot sting of daylight; harsh, unfiltered.

Vehicle? Yes, though the angles are all wrong, I'm staring *down* at the Plexiglass sidings of some sort of cabin, tipping forward in my chair at approximately forty five degrees. I'm not sat; I'm *hanging*.

Reality bites – literally – the chill air gnawing at the exposed skin of my hands and face. I'm still wearing Oscar's jumper, though now it is sodden and clings to my upper body like a wet towel.

I'm aching in places that it isn't wise to ache. My head feels like its been hollowed out and repacked with ground rubble. For a half-minute or so I just exist, squinting out into space, the seatbelt continuing its slow cheese-wiring of my shoulder, parched tongue lolling out past cracked lips.

There's a low creaking sound as the vehicle tilts forward a couple of degrees. Wherever we are it isn't stable. Reaching out I run my fingertips over long black gear sticks with balled handles, a king-sized steering wheel. Speed and petrol dials, smeared in dust. A filthy dashboard bearing a faded sticker with the crest of the Manchester United football team.

Okay then.

So I'm in Jed de Gruchy's JCB earth mover.

And not just *in it*, but *hanging off a cliff in it*, the view through the windscreen resolving itself into a hundred foot drop towards dark, jagged rocks and equally unappealing waters. Waves pound furiously below, flinging huge plumes of spray up to splatter noisily against the cabin's Plexiglass flanks. The tide is high and hungry.

Where's Michael Caine when you need him? The vehicle creaks again, this time shifting to the left a little, the sly moans and murmurs that escape the metal betraying its slow creep forwards. Trying to ignore the collective howl of my various discomforts I begin to assess my options.

The digger appears to have gone over the cliff edge face first, though the teeth of its lowered metal bucket have caught beneath a solid looking hummock of earth on the way down. It's done a good job, that hummock, though even hummocks tire; as I watch the bucket bites a little further into the earth, the whole digger tipping another inch towards the drop. Any moment now and something's going to give.

Swivelling my bloated melon of a head up over the blare of my left shoulder I see that I'm about fifteen feet down from the headland, a flattened gash of ripped and matted foliage marking the digger's path down to the ledge on which it has lodged. Above this straggled lip the early morning sky sulks bleached and sunless.

Whoops. I shouldn't have swivelled like that; the digger responds to my displaced weight by lurching forward an inch or two, snapping my big ball of hurty head down on to my chest. I hear the bucket's teeth crunching their way through the earth, hear the eager smashing of the waves below.

Out. Now. I reach for the seatbelt release, find that I'm not even clipped in, merely tangled with the thing. This is good news. Once freed I should be able to climb through the door and get Bear Grylls with the cliff face. It's this first movement that gives me pause; the necessary lunge forwards towards the scoop and that crumbling bookend of dirt.

Come on, damn it. Out.

There's a thud above as a seagull lands on the cabin roof. Dirty great thing it is, its black eye fixed on me through the plastic, head cocked as though waiting for a response.

The earth mover creaks forward a few inches more.

Crunching of rock, squeal of metal.

The seagull takes a runny crap before reeling away with a squawk. As commentaries go that's pretty apt.

Let's do this, I mutter, moving as quickly as my battered limbs allow. The cabin door – mercifully unlatched – swings outwards at the push of my palm, though my left foot gets caught between the gear sticks on its way past.

The JCB lurches forward with a hideous metal wail. Below the grey water flexes and flings, the white spume its fingers, eager to grip and crush.

I manage to wriggle my foot loose at the expense of one of Oscar's trainers, which tumbles from the cabin, bouncing twice off the rock face on its way down. I'm out now, numb fingers thrust into cracks in the rock, wet soil crumbling over my knuckles. Clambering free from the cabin I scrabble out on to the cliff face, my extended left foot moving in a curious little dance as it seeks purchase. *Wanted: foothold of solid rock, no time wasters please.*

Got one. Up now. Face full of spiky wet nature. Fingers merely mangled blobs of pain and cold. Up some more, reaching out for the lip of the land, hauling myself via gathered ropes of grass, stem and weed. Brambles rip at the white meat of my wrists. I taste the metal blare of soil in my mouth, feel it crunching between my teeth.

Beside me the JCB continues to creak forwards, its tracks somehow maintaining their grip on the ledge. I'm clear of it now though, so go on then you big metal bastard, *fall*. A big, pointless explosion please, with orange flames blooming, repeated impact shots from a variety of angles, the works. After you. Whenever you're ready.

But no. The digger just hangs there. Creaking. Clicking. Peering down at the water like some suicidal robot, a Transformer grown sick of transforming yet worried lest it won't know how to drown. Worried it'll just sit there on the bottom getting cold and wet and rusty until someone can be bothered to winch it out.

Turning my back for good on the metal yellow misery I drag myself kicking and clawing up the final few feet of incline, back on to solid land, finally hauling myself over and up on to my knees.

It doesn't take long to work out where I am. I'm back at Corbet's Folly – where else? – though the landscape has changed significantly since my last visit.

Something's happened to old Moses' home.

I drag myself a few more metres clear of the cliff edge, following the thick muddy treads carved by the digger on its way down the field, up to what's left of the tower. For where once the lopsided structure stood there is now an ugly pile of rubble, as though someone has taken a huge steel-capped toe – or a JCB earth mover, even – to its landward side and just kept on kicking. Most of the sea-facing outer wall remains, as does the rear portion of the first floor (from where I see my lino flapping), though the rest of the structure has simply caved in upon itself. Now, with its charred, empty innards bared to the rising light Corbet's Folly cuts a sorry sight, like some half stamped-on snail in urgent need of a merciful heel.

Did I do this? What the hell happened last night? Closing my eyes I plunge my hands into the mental slurry. On the fringes of my recollection are The Lamplighter, Babs, those pints...tequila, yes at some point we discussed the likelihood of one of us objecting should the other suggest we order tequila, but *then...*?

Nothing.

Welcome back to Blanksville. Population: one.

On my feet now, staggering like some sad inverted Robinson Crusoe back up and on to the desert island of his birth. Reaching a large granite slab I pitch forward, my cheek rapidly becoming one with the numbing chill of the stone. I roll groaning on to my back, exposing myself to the paper-white emptiness of the sky like some upturned shellfish with its pale belly bared. Come gulls, devour. Memories from yesterday surface and break, woven phantasms of faces, fading swirls of motion, echoes of pain and anger and confusion and loss.

Chadwick. O'Malley. Shah.

Louise.

Oh God. Louise.

Daddy can I?

Somewhere off in the distance something tears free with a monstrous shriek, succumbing at last to the pull of its fate, crashing buckled and bent into the depths. Jed's digger, I'm guessing, though more than that, more...something inside of me has come loose too...

Daddy can I?

My makeshift tombstone cold and hard against my back, the last remnants of mania oozing from the shattered shell of my being (for yesterday I have been manic and today I fear I will not be so) I suddenly see things for what they are, and what they have been, and how they are likely to proceed. Somewhere in that painted sky of mine a black crack has appeared – an *antilight* – an infinite and terrifyingly familiar vacuum from which only the obliterating crush of Oblivion's boot can save me.

Come gulls, devour. Pick me clean. I'm yours.

Can I go now?

Can I...please...can I...

...go swimming, please? Daddy can I...

24 – Twist

'...go swimming?'

Of course she can. Whatever. So long as she leaves Daddy in peace on his towel (with his little secret tucked away beneath its flowery folds) she can do what she wants, bless her. Just don't be heading back up the beach to the car park. And make sure to stay in the shallows.

We've given up on making sandcastles, mutually angered by the fine white sand's unwillingness to cohere. And it's too hot for racket ball, and Daddy's not feeling all that great (though it's certainly warmer here then that other place he was a moment ago) so he'd rather just lie here for a bit, if that's okay. At least until he works out where he is.

Well go on then, darling. Go swimming. Leave Daddy alone for a bit with his buried bottle (warm vodka, yuck) and his straw. Here on his front with his head lowered where no-one can see him slurpslurpslurping – the mums and their toddlers and those long-legged teenage girls over by the slipway – no-one need know of Daddy's shame.

But *is* it shame? Is it really? Or is it simply Daddy's way of getting through the day, of angling the nose cone of that ever-buckling spacecraft of his away from the black hole in his head that keeps on threatening to sucksucksuck him in. He's more fun when he's got this stuff in him. Better company for you, Louise. Better company for everyone.

Just a few more slurps, a minute or two in this sun and Daddy's coming down to the waterline to check that you're okay. And when the screaming starts around him, when people start leaping to their feet and yelling for help and pointing at the little pink thing being rolled in on the waves then maybe Daddy will wake up and realise that he's WAKE UP and realise that I'm...

...drowning, on my back, on a freezing granite slab. No more warm soft sand. No more heat of beach. No, Louise has gone and the sky has collapsed and I'm dying, suffocating beneath wet fabric as a torrent of filthy water pours down above. Whenever I gasp or snort or buck it's there, filling my nostrils, splattering heavily over my face, blocking the mute scream of my mouth like an acrid liquid pillow. I'm drowning, drowning like my daughter

Honey I'm coming I'm coming

and any second now I'm going to die. I keep struggling – plain old instinct insists – and thrashing my head, but a tight pressure grips me firm at either temple, leans heavily on my chest. Above me, through the weave of the fabric I can make out the two snarling faces of my attackers as the deluge continues – it's *lager*, I realise, I'm drowning in the most horrible lager – as my lungs explode and a heavy, creeping blackness enfolds...

'GOOD MORNING MR DARK!'

There's a sudden break in my lagerboarding; the wet cloth is pulled free from my face, allowing me to drag the sky into my lungs in huge, wracking gasps. Howe's gloved palms press hard against my shoulders as he pins me wriggling to the granite slab, his snarling face leering into focus, eyes sparkling with a relish as black as his attire.

An open can of Tennent's Pilsner hangs in the air above me, the next tide of golden torture set to spill. Beyond that, a brown hand flashing gold at the knuckles, the arm of a dark red leather jacket, a buttoned collar atop which the rounded jowls of Hassan Shah split into a wide bullfrog grin.

'HOW ARE WE DOING?'

I struggle, but Howe's too strong. I'm bound, too; several elastic bungee cords have been wrapped around my chest, their plastic hooks entwined beneath the granite slab. It's the same deal just above my knees.

This all feels oddly familiar.

'Round two!' laughs Shah, laying the wet towel over my nose and mouth before I've a chance to summon the phlegm required to decorate his face. Tennent's tumbles. Cue pain, struggling, throat burn, spluttering, consciousness of drowning and fighting the drowning whilst hoping the drowning just drowns me etc. I'm too busy enduring it to worry about description.

They must have a stack of cans, as through the pain I can hear the tiny crunch of the next one being opened as each one runs out and is replaced. Eventually it stops, Shah scrunching the final empty can in his hand and bouncing it off my forehead as I gasp for air through the sodden cloth.

'Back seat. Two more crates.' The officer moves off, leaving a big expanse of grey, Howe-less sky behind him. Having peeled the cloth from my face Shah squats, bringing his fat mouth level with my ear.

'There's a fresh bottle of Macallan as well,' he sneers. 'I'd planned it is a gift in return for those papers. In return for walking away from all this and leaving me to get on with my tower. And then I find out about...*this*.'

'You like...' I manage, between gasps. 'You like...what I've done with the place?'

Shah's smug face creases, white teeth bared behind the thick curl of his lips.

'You pathetic drunken *bum*,' he spits. 'All you had to do was walk away. All you had to do was leave me to it.'

'Now where's the f...fun in that?'

The wide canopy of Shah's face leans in close, nostrils flaring. I smell the spice of his hot, spittle-flecked breath on my cheeks. 'Officer Howe informs me that you've been in touch with some of his colleagues. That you've been passing on certain information. Not a clever move.'

'Not clever at all,' says Howe, returning from wherever with a plastic-wrapped slab of Tennent's Pilsner tucked under each arm.

'You'll be glad to know I've already picked the car park they're going to find you in, once I'm gone,' Shah continues. 'Sixth floor, in case you're wondering. Lovely little spot by the lift. You might even make the news. Little Louise will be *so* upset. But don't worry. Officer Howe here will make sure to break it to her...*gently*.'

I lunge upwards, the bungee cord cutting into my chest as Howe's palms descend, slamming me back down on the granite slab. Shah lifts the cloth – a Harp beer towel, I see now – and slaps the sodden fabric down over my face. Off we go again, a fresh deluge ushering me swiftly off to the edge of oblivion.

Tennent's, I find myself bewailing through the agony. Of all the beers in the world to drown in, why *Tennent's,* for Christ's sake? And as for Harp; do they even still *make* that stuff?

Somewhere at the edge of the cosmos a voice rings out, my own, possibly, a farewell of sorts. The light dims, funnelling to a tiny point, receding. This is it – I've passed over, my soul tumbling like spat offal down a beer-slick tunnel, down into the stale depths of some rancid liquid underworld. The pain is indescribable, cellular, every filament of my being crying out for release but finding none. So this is Hell then – I've finally arrived – splashing down into my own personal lake of low percentage brimstone to see out eternity in a frothing torment of pain and regret and cheap, watery pish.

The End.

Only it isn't.

This isn't the end, and this is not quite Hell. The universe lists; I'm falling – physically falling – and then the ground is under me, striking at my knees, blunting my elbows. Somehow I'm able to roll over on to my back as blurred giants wrestle above me beneath a crying iron sky.

Huge fists are hurled. Celestial voices boom.

'Up, Goldie! Up!'

I do what I'm told, rolling across the dirt and pushing myself up on to all fours, the cold air hacking at my lungs, stale lager pouring from the various holes of my face. I look up to see Oscar de Gruchy gripping Howe in a headlock. The officer's feet scuffle and slide on the wet grass as he tries to wriggle free; his face has turned a bright and brilliant purple as he swings his right fist wildly, attempting to land blows against the side of Oscar's head.

Shah's backed off, palms raised in a gesture of surrender, face taut with panic as Jed de Gruchy – yelling furious in his Man Utd shirt – races over from the car park, having just leapt from his brother's jeep. Jed seems less concerned with Oscar's scuffle and more bothered by the twin tracks of tire-flattened earth leading off towards the cliff top, for upon seeing these he stops dead, his hands on his head.

'*Goldie!* Do something!'

Oscar drops to one knee, bringing Howe down with him. The officer's eyes gaze wildly out from the purpled pudding of his face. I should go and punch him or something. Kick him in the groin. Tweak his nipples. I should do all this and more, but I can't. My lungs are too raw, my breath too ragged for my body to be of use.

'DARK! The gun!'

Howe's Glock. He's making a last gasp play for it, slapping desperately at his hip in an attempt to snatch the weapon from its holster. For a moment he has it, until a rough jerk from Oscar loosens his grip. The Glock falls to the grass and soon Howe goes with it, his eyes rolling over, his body becoming limp. Oscar maintains the headlock all the way, lowering the unconscious officer to the ground.

Which just leaves Hassan Shah. Palms bared and quivering, eyes flashing panic he takes several steps back towards the ruined wall of the tower. And panic he should, for here comes Jed, racing across the field, one fist raised and ready to smite.

'You okay Goldie?' says Oscar, helping me to my feet.

I manage a nod, of sorts.

'My digger!' yells Jed, punching me squarely in the face. It's a real beauty, as blows go. Nice and clean. No breakages, no speech bubbled THWACKS or KAPOWS, just a swift, solid impact that sends me sprawling back to the dirt where I belong.

'My fucking digger! You drove my digger off a fucking cliff!'

I did.

'He's not a happy boy, Dark,' says Oscar, helping me up. 'Spotted it was gone this morning. Sprayed his muesli everywhere. Following you was easy enough seeing as you hit pretty much every tree, car and building on your way...' he motions over at the cliff edge where Jed is squatting, head in hands, '...down there.'

'Mr Shah!'

We turn. Bella Brice stands at the edge of the car park, next to the brothers' jeep, a silver sports car (Shah's, I assume) and her own still-idling Porsche. 'Stop!' she yells, palms raised high as though attempting to halt an oncoming bus. 'Hassan! No!'

We turn again. Shah's holding the Glock at arm's length, its snub nose sniffing me out for the second time in as many days.

'Woah there.' Oscar raises his hands in surrender. Jed too.

'Officer Howe!' Shah steps forward to administer a firm kick to the prone man's side, keeping the handgun held firmly out before him. 'Officer Howe! Get up!'

Howe stirs, groggily raising a hand to his crushed throat.

'My commiserations, Mr Dark.' A mad grin splits the Arab's jowls. The wind has ruffled his hair, flinging it in slick strands across his forehead. 'Your miserable life continues. And as for you, farmer boy...assaulting a police officer...never wise.'

Oscar frowns down at Howe, up at me.

'Police?' He grimaces.

I nod. *Afraid so.*

'You think this little act of vandalism bothers me?' Shah tips his head towards the rubble-strewn gash in the side Corbet's Tower. 'You think this little tantrum of yours has *achieved* anything? I could build five of these if I wanted. Like *that*. And I probably will. Glass ones. Metal ones. A whole row of them. Because I have the *means*, Mr Dark. Like it or not, money rules this precious island of yours, as it does the world, and I shall do as I please! So have another drink on me, my friend. Raise a toast to Mr Chadwick and his ilk whilst you're at it. I should imagine the fish will have had their fill of him by now. He could probably do with cheering up.'

Howe hobbles uneasily to his feet, one hand on the back of his neck. He spits blood, eying Oscar all the while.

'Mr Shah!' Brice's call is urgent. 'We need to go.' The thin wail of a siren slices through the mist from somewhere off towards the road. Shah stiffens at the sound, Howe nervously glancing inland. I turn to the de Gruchy boys, who shrug in unison. Not their doing.

'Fuck.' No sooner has the word left Howe's mouth then he turns and starts stumbling across the grass towards the car park. Brice is already climbing back into her Porsche. Shah remains where he is, staring down in surprise at the Glock like someone just magicked it into his hands. Then he too turns and follows Howe over the field, his fat jowls bouncing.

Too late. The police cars – two of them – are already pulling in, their roof lights flicking reds and blues across the grey vista as they crunch to a stop on the gravel.

'This your doing, Goldie?' asks Oscar.

I respond by bending double and vomiting over his boots.

Oscar sighs.

Shah and Howe reach the car park as three uniformed officers spring from the first car and start barking orders. Howe's hands go up. More shouts; *hands on the bonnet! on the bonnet!*

Shah complies with a slow shake of the head. He's lost the Glock. Must have ditched it in the grass.

A familiar face floats free from the second car. Iain Ledger stands tall, sniffs the air to the intro bars of his own inner theme tune, opening credits rolling boldly through his head. As the yellow jackets of the officers converge around Shah's party Super Mario breaks his pose to come striding across the field towards us with a face like smashed granite.

'Jesus, Oscar.' Jed runs an anxious hand through his hair. 'You just put a copper in a sleeper hold. A fucking *copper*.'

A rogue one, working alone, I want to tell them, though the words freeze in my mouth. Because the truth is I'm not so sure. I'm not so sure of anything right now.

'Stay right there, prick,' yells Ledger, as I step forward with outstretched arms and vomit-spattered chin. 'Stay right where ye fucking are. You two.' He indicates Oscar and Jed with alternate jabs of the index finger. 'Over there please. I'll be speakin' tae you boys in a minute.'

The de Gruchys slouch off towards the car park, where Howe can be heard loudly holding forth to his fellow officers with animated gestures, several of them aimed my way. A few feet away Shah – standing now, with arms folded – and Brice watch on, the latter already whispering instructions into her client's ear.

'You want ta tell me what the holy hell's been going on here, Mr Private fucking Investigator?' Ledger steps in close but quickly backs away, swatting at his nose. 'For *fuck*'s sake, Dark. You smell like a brewery specialisin' in bottled shit. I've a mind to arrest you for the pure stink alone. And that's just fer starters.'

'Good to see you, Iain.'

'Is it now?'

I really hope so. But are those Shah's millions I see glinting in the corners of Ledger's eyes? Is that the Arab's signature I detect upon the thin line of his smile? I'm sunk if so.

Over in the car park the situation is unfolding, and I'm not sure I like it. Howe's continuing to point my way, explaining something to one of the officers, his hands busy. She nods, her hands on her hips. Yes, her body language seems to be saying. *Yes, I understand.*

'So then,' says Ledger. 'Here we are again. Or rather, here *you* are again.'

I've never been a big gambler – not for *money*, in any case – though I did indulge in the odd card game back in my university days. Pontoon was a favourite of ours, though I was never any good. Never knew when to stop twisting. Nineteen, twenty – on I'd go. Expecting an ace, getting a face.

Let's play.

'Shah had Bill O'Malley killed,' I wheeze. 'He wanted the tower. O'Malley was going to help him get it. Then he wasn't.'

Twist.

'Is that right? And what would a fucking multi-millionaire want with a pile of wonky shite like this?' Ledger waves at the blocky wreckage of Corbet's Folly '*Before* you smashed it down, that is.'

Over in the car park Howe has placed a placatory hand laid on the officer's shoulder. Old friends, clearly. Worse, Brice is on the phone, making reassuring gestures to Shah as he rests lightly on to the bonnet of the Porsche, his arms still folded, his dark eyes seeking me out across the grass.

The de Gruchys are having their rights read to them.

My gut sinks.

I meet Shah's gaze. He raises a hand, twinkling his fingers at me like a coy schoolgirl, his grin spreading.

'Well, Dark?'

'Because he's insane, Iain.'

'Unlike you.'

'Howe shot Chadwick.' My throat cracks and I cough painfully. Deep breath. Got to get this out. 'Body's in a bag at the bottom of St Aubin's bay. Weapon's round here somewhere. I'll help you find it. A Glock.'

Twist.

'Is that so?' Ledger leans in closer, his face a mockery of false incredulity, moustache and eyebrows moving upwards as one. 'A Glock, hey? Wow.'

'There's an answer phone recording of Howe threatening to shoot me with it. In the knee. Yesterday. Before he forced us onto *The Sabre*. I can get it for you.'

Twist.

'Goodness me.' Ledger folds his arms behind his back. Turning his head he squints off into the inscrutable grey wash of the Channel as though searching for the horizon. Howe's laugh floats over from the car park, tremulous, high. The de Gruchys are being guided into the back of the police car.

And there's Shah again. Catching my eye he gives a theatrical bow; right arm tight to his belly, left hand descending in a slow flourish, fingers jiggling as it completes its arc.

'Is that so?' mutters Ledger, chewing his lip, still gazing out over the waves. And then he nods to himself, just once, as though ticking some internal box.

'You're a fuckin' prick, Dark,' he calls over his shoulder. 'You know that? A waste o' fuckin' space. I need to know you know that. Yes?'

'Yes.'

'Good.'

And then Ledger turns and waves over at the car park and everything changes. In an instant two officers are on Howe, thrusting him face first over the roof of the Porsche as the one tending to Oscar and Jed suddenly switches her attention to Shah, simultaneously dipping her head and barking into the walkie-talkie pinned to her jacket. There's scuffling, shouts. Things get a little ugly. Shah is spun and searched.

Stick.

I exhale noisily. Didn't even realise I was holding my breath. And with that release of stale air comes something else; a wave of dizziness, the unheard crunch of something snapping in my brain. Thick inner curtains part and there's that black hole again, its destroying un-light at once flooding every niche and rumple of my brain. I stagger as though struck, glance around me for anything with which to extinguish the dark fire roaring through my mind.

The slab of Tennent's. Where is it? Got to be some cans left.

'You're still nicked for this shite by the way,' says Ledger, gesturing at the tumbled tower. 'But thanks for the rest. Had to wait and see what you were going to offer up by way of evidence before I pressed ahead wi' that lot over there.'

'*Howe.*' Or 'how?' I'm not sure anymore. Not sure of anything. Did I even say that? The word floats away from me like a bubble. I've found the rest of Shah's lager. Cracking a can I lift it to my lips only to have Ledger smash it from my hand.

'Fuck's sake man! I'm talking tae you! D'ye remember staggerin' into the station late last night and demandin' to speak wi' Jan?'

'No.' I definitely say the word this time, though not in response to Ledger. I say NO because I can feel it all collapsing around me, the barriers and the scaffolds with which I've been propping myself these past few months, this whole ridiculous pretence. I yell NO to the black hole in my head, even as the vortex widens to swallow me whole.

'Aye. Right. Anyhow, you unloaded the whole fuckin' story. Handed over all yer bits. Said you were off to put it right. Jan was all set to take you in for the night until you started bangin' on about me an her, ya wee bastard, which – by the way – you ever fuckin' *mention* again and I'll rip your spine out, right?'

Daddy can I go swimming?

No, sweetheart. Not today. Because we're going home now. Daddy's taking you home to your mummy and then he's going to get help. Look what he's brought on to the beach with him! Silly Daddy. Let's pour it into the sand shall we...make one final sandcastle with it before we go...

'Anyway, so Jan phones me and fills me in. Superhero that I am I hit the station at five am – I'm guessing round about the same time as you're driving a stolen JCB around the lanes – and do some diggin' of mah own. Truth told we've had a file open on Shah since he got here. Certain irregularities...'

'Give my love to your daughter, Dark!'

I look up towards the source of the voice.

No.

A gigantic bullfrog squats atop the roof of one of the police cars, its smile as wide as its body. Dark eyes widen, glinting. It winks.

We're going home, Louise.

The world lists like a sinking liner and I drop to one knee, shaking my head in an attempt to clear the dizziness. No good – event horizon has been reached – I'm folding in and over on myself, crumpling and tearing and coming apart.

No.

I have a responsibility.

I have purpose.

I have a reason to be here.

'Protection,' I hear myself mumbling, reaching out to Ledger. 'For Louise. I want protection for my daughter.'

'Marigold...'

'*Protection.*'

'For god's sake, man, get up...'

'Please. *Please*. For Louise.'

Reality's awhirl now, a hundred spinning Ledgers – *let's not go through this again*, he's saying – I'm up on my feet, tears flowing freely, screaming my daughter's name – *he doesn't know, Dark*, reaching for my elbow, *probably just seen those old pictures you keep puttin' up on Facebook*...but I snatch myself clear of his grip, turning instead to the shattered wreckage of Corbet's Folly, staggering towards its scorched brick innards, the world falling silent and still and perfectly focused as I see him – Moses Corbet – his buckled back, his tattered robes, his long white beard...I see him peering from one of the window slits, forehead to the cooling stone, gazing out at the Channel with sad, tired eyes, praying for the slightest sign of even the smallest French vessel upon the waves...days, weeks and months he stares, as the moss creeps and the rain leaks and the mortar crumbles and his body weakens, whole decades spent staring out upon that cruel, unyielding sea in the hope that one day Redemption will bare her sails...and he sees me too *he sees me too!* the skin on his wispy skull tightening in excitement, his eyes finally finding their light, those thin lips parting to form the echo of a smile:

I see her, he mouths. *I see her. Louise.*

('For god's sake, Dark!' the lawman's voice rings out from somewhere far away, 'she's been gone two years now! Dark...get back here now!')

But we see her, truly we do, and as our battered bodies tip to greet her our legs are forced to match their lunge, propelling us along in great staggering strides towards the edge of the cliff – there's a boat approaching, *they're back!* and she's waving, *Louise*! – through the tears and the laughter and the audible fizzing of our brains the little girl is smiling and waving at her

Daddy, her wet hair plastered across her face, a chewed Little Mermaid figure in her hands and we're waving too – *man the alarms!* – we're waving too as the brambles applaud our passing and the ground starts to crumble as though the island itself is urging us on and the lawman's words still reach us and he almost gets a hold of our collar but we're coming *Louise!* we've seen, we're forgiven, we'll get there this time, just these last few rocks to go just that final mound to launch from and we're up and we're over and we're gone, we're gone, I'm gone.

ABOUT THE AUTHOR

Paul Bisson was born on the Channel Island of Jersey in 1976. He studied English at Liverpool University and taught in North London for several years before returning to his native rock in 2005. An aspiring novelist in his spare time, he earns his bread as a college lecturer and semi-professional musician.

Marigold Dark is his second novel.

Contact Paul via **email** at pbisson32@hotmail.com

Visit his **website** at www.paulbisson.com

Twitter: @LeBiss

From the same author...

COYOTE JACK AND THE BLUEBIRDS

The Bluebirds have hit the jackpot.

Celebrity Texas blues star Coyote Jack has agreed to join the band for a one night show at their home venue in Jersey. But the bluesman's erratic behaviour soon sparks concern, and it isn't long before the Bluebirds begin to suspect that their wings may have been clipped for good. It's up to singer Charlie French to pull the band together and unravel the mystery of Coyote Jack as the clock ticks down to their final gig, where an eager crowd awaits...

'a delightful tale' - A. Kearney, Amazon reviewer

'a paean to the art of live blues music' - M.Todaro, Amazon reviewer

AVAILABLE ON AMAZON

From the same author...

MUDDY WATERS ATE MY WIFE!

A novelette

July, 1980. Legendary Chicago bluesman Muddy Waters and his band have arrived in the Channel Islands to play a one night gig at Fort Regent, Jersey. Local guitar hero Norman Peacock is as excited as any man, until he learns of Waters' intention to seal a decades-old diabolical deal via the oral consumption of Norman's wife.

Now Norman must maintain his strut against dark, gathering forces as he mounts the ramparts for a climactic and sanity-shattering showdown with Waters and his henchmen...

'Quirky, witty and original' - Glover Wright, author of *Aurora*

'Brilliantly executed' - John Hanley, author of *Against the Tide*

AVAILABLE ON AMAZON

Printed in Great Britain
by Amazon.co.uk, Ltd.,
Marston Gate.